The First

The 18th Donut Mystery

From *New York Times* Bestselling Author

Jessica Beck

DANGEROUS DOUGH

Other Books by Jessica Beck

The Donut Shop Mysteries

Glazed Murder
Fatally Frosted
Sinister Sprinkles
Evil Éclairs
Tragic Toppings
Killer Crullers
Drop Dead Chocolate
Powdered Peril
Illegally Iced
Deadly Donuts
Assault and Batter
Sweet Suspects
Deep Fried Homicide
Custard Crime
Lemon Larceny
Bad Bites
Old Fashioned Crooks
Dangerous Dough

The Classic Diner Mysteries

A Chili Death
A Deadly Beef
A Killer Cake
A Baked Ham
A Bad Egg
A Real Pickle
A Burned Biscuit

The Ghost Cat Cozy Mysteries

Ghost Cat: Midnight Paws

Ghost Cat 2: Bid for Midnight

Jessica Beck is the *New York Times* bestselling author of the Donut Shop Mysteries from St. Martin's Press and Author of the Classic Diner Mystery Series and the Ghost Cat Cozy Mysteries from Cozy Publishing.

To you, my loyal readers,
this is the one you've been asking for!

Dangerous Dough by Jessica Beck; Copyright © 2015

Chapter 1

A honeymoon, by its very definition, isn't supposed to last forever, but I wished that mine with Jake had been longer than the week we spent together in Paris after our hurried nuptials. Flying back to North Carolina's Charlotte Douglas Airport was bittersweet after the wondrous time we'd spent exploring the City of Lights hand in hand as a freshly minted married couple, but the glow was suddenly extinguished when we got back to my Jeep in the long-term parking lot and found my mother there waiting for us.

I knew instantly that there was trouble—that much was obvious from her face—but I didn't have any idea just how much until she told us the real reason she was there.

Chapter 2
Eight Days Earlier

"Can't you do that any faster?" Jake asked me as I finished making out the day's deposit slip. He'd just proposed and I'd readily accepted, but that didn't mean that I could drop everything and just go. After all, Donut Hearts needed to be taken care of before I could leave.

"I'm working as fast as I can," I told him with a grin. "Who knew that you could be so impatient?"

"I'm afraid that if I give you too much time to think about it, you might change your mind," he said with a smile matching my own.

"There's not a chance in the world of that happening, mister," I said after I took the time to give him a quick peck on the lips. "You're not getting rid of me that easily."

"That's good, because I feel the same way about you." He frowned for a moment before he spoke again. "Don't forget, you need to call Emma."

"As much as she means to me, I'm not inviting her to our wedding, Jake. If I ask more folks than Momma and Grace to be our witnesses, where do I draw the line? Do we have to invite Chief Martin? How about your friend Terry Hanlan? Can we exclude Emily Hargraves? If we invite her, then what about Max? I don't know about you, but I'd rather not have my ex-husband attending my wedding, but that's not all. What is Gabby Williams going to say if we invite the others but we exclude her? Before we know it, it's going to be completely out of control. Don't worry; Emma will understand."

"I'm not talking about the ceremony, Suzanne. You need to ask her to take over the donut shop while we're gone."

"You're right," I said with a laugh as I reached for the phone. "That's something I really have to take care of before we take off. Let me call her right now."

"Hang on a second," Jake said as he put a hand on mine. "We need to figure something out first. Are you going to tell her the real reason we won't be here for the next week?" "Why not? We're getting married, and I want the whole world to know," I answered with a smile. I couldn't help it. Grinning now seemed to be my resting face. "Well, they certainly all will if you tell Emma the truth. Can you imagine Ray Blake not putting it on the front page of his newspaper? Last week he ran a headline about the volunteer fire department getting a cat out of a tree. I've got a feeling that he's going to think this is a lot more newsworthy than that."

"Let him," I said, "unless you don't want folks to know." "He can put it on a billboard for all I care," Jake said. "I just wanted to make sure that you were okay with it. Go on. Make the call."

"Isn't there someone else you need to call yourself?" I asked him before I dialed Emma's number.

"Not me. I'm all set. George will be ready for us at one, Grace and your mother are on standby, I've made our plane reservations for seven tonight, and we're staying a week at a quaint little place on the Isle de Saint Louis that a guy on the force recommended."

"Where exactly is that in Paris?" I asked him.

"Trust me; you're going to love it. It's on an island in the Seine, the one right next to Notre Dame. I checked it out a month ago online, and it looks awesome."

That was touching, since I'd told him time and time again that I'd wanted to go to Paris all my life. Who knew that he'd actually been listening? "You already looked into it? Jake, how long have you been planning this honeymoon?"

He grinned sheepishly at me. "To tell you the truth, I was planning to take you anyway; going there on our honeymoon sounded like a perfect excuse to me." As he was saying it, he must have realized how that sounded, because he quickly added, "Not that I need an excuse to go anywhere with you."

I had to laugh. "Don't worry about how it sounded.

Today, of all days, you get a Get Out of Jail Free card from me. After all, it's our wedding day."

"It is at that," he said, and then he frowned slightly. "Does that mean that it's bad luck for me to see you before the ceremony?"

I kissed him again before I replied. At that rate, I was never going to get my deposit done, but who cared? I was getting married! "As far as I'm concerned, it's *never* bad luck when I see you." I made the call, swore Emma to secrecy first, and then told her our news.

"You're getting married!" she shrieked happily. "That's wonderful."

"Emma, you can tell your father, but could you at least wait until three o'clock this afternoon?"

"Sure, but why the delay?" my young assistant asked.

"Because the ceremony will be over by then." I hesitated, and then I knew I had to tell her that she wasn't invited to the nuptials. "You know that you are one of my dearest friends, but we're just having two witnesses today, and there will be no guests at all. Can you forgive me for excluding you?"

She laughed at the news, which was a good sign. "Suzanne, I'd think you were insane if you did it any other way! If Grace or your mother can't make it, you can call me to be a witness, but otherwise, you have my blessing not to invite me."

"How did you know they'd be our witnesses?" I asked her.

"Who else would you ask? Mom and I will be delighted to step in at the shop while you're gone. I'm assuming you're going on a honeymoon, aren't you?"

"Jake is taking me to Paris," I said happily.

"Mom's going to be jealous that you're going to France and she isn't."

"To tell you the truth, I still can't believe that it's happening," I said.

"Well, don't worry about Donut Hearts for one second. She'll be in good hands."

"I know she will," I said. "Thanks."

"It's truly wonderful news, Suzanne," Emma said happily.
"It is, isn't it?" I replied, and then I hung up. "It's all set," I told Jake.
"Good," he replied. "*Now* are you finished?"
Thank goodness the money we took in balanced the first time I ran my report. If it hadn't, I wasn't sure that I would have even cared. "I'm ready to go," I said.
"Then let's get out of here. We can pack our bags and leave right after the ceremony," Jake said.
"Why the rush? Our flight doesn't leave until seven, so we'll have plenty of time to make it."
"I'm trying to avoid anyone making a fuss over us," he admitted.
I had to laugh. "We both know that's not happening. Momma's going to insist that we have some kind of celebration before we go. You can bank on it."
Jake's brow furrowed for an instant. "Suzanne, we don't really need to share this moment with anyone else, do we?"
I patted his arm gently. "Do you honestly think it would be for us? It's just Momma's way of saying she's pleased with our decision, and she wants the world to know it."
"Maybe it will just be a few people," Jake said.
My groom could believe that if he wanted, but I knew in my heart that he was delusional.
My mother was many things, but low profile wasn't one of them.

To my great surprise and relief, there wasn't a huge crowd waiting for us when we got to the courthouse. Jake must have sensed a shift in my mood, because he glanced over at me. "You're not having second thoughts, are you?"
"Not on your life. I was half expecting a mob to be here waiting for us, though. In all honesty, I'm kind of relieved that no one else is here."
He patted my arm gently. "Your mother is respecting our wishes."
"I know. That's what is so crazy about it. Maybe they're

all waiting inside to ambush us."

Jake's laughter was infectious, and I found myself joining him. "Suzanne, are you ready to do this?"

"Always and forever."

I was happy to see Momma and Grace waiting just inside the door for us. After a round of quick hugs, I told my mother, "Thank you so much."

"For being here? You know that I wouldn't have missed it for the world."

"Sure, for that, but most of all for not making this a mob scene."

"I know how to show restraint when it's called for," Momma said a little diffidently, and then she smiled at me. "Shall we?"

The four of us made our way to the mayor's office, and again, I held my breath as Jake opened the door.

I was relieved to see that our officiant was alone. Dressed in his finest suit, the mayor smiled broadly as we entered.

"Let's get this thing rolling, folks. You've got a plane to catch," George said with a hearty grin. "Are you both ready?"

"We are," Jake and I said in perfect unison, as though we'd practiced beforehand.

George's grin broadened. "That's what I like: a couple in perfect synch."

The mayor moved in front of his desk as Jake and I joined him there. Momma and Grace were just a few steps back, but it felt as though no one else in the world was there but my fiancé and me. Jake squeezed my hand, and then he winked at me as I turned toward him. I smiled back, and we moved to face George together.

As the mayor finished reading from his script, I saw that there were a few errant tears in George's eyes, though they were difficult to see through my own. Jake wiped absently at his own cheek, and I was certain that if I looked backward,

Momma and Grace would be weeping as well. There was no sadness in any of it today; they were all tears of joy, and I welcomed them, a proper beginning for the new life that Jake and I were embarking on.

"Go on. Kiss your bride," George urged as he finished the ceremony, and Jake took me in his arms and did just that. The applause behind us was lost on me.

I had myself a brand-new husband, and I couldn't have been happier about it.

Once we had all signed the documents George had laid out for us, I turned to my new husband. "Just think. Tomorrow we'll be together in Paris."

"I'm starting to think that you might have married me just for the honeymoon." He reddened a little before he added, "You know what I mean. I'm talking about the trip."

I kissed his cheek. "Of course you are."

My mother coughed a bit to get my attention. "Suzanne, there's something you both need to see before you go anywhere. It's important."

I knew this was just her way of trying to whisk us off to whatever festivities she'd planned for us, but I didn't have to make it easy on her. "What could possibly be that important to us today, of all days?" I asked her.

"Come downstairs to the basement with me and you'll see," she said. I recognized that enigmatic smile, and I knew that something was about to happen.

"You arranged some kind of reception for us, didn't you?" I asked her.

"Now, don't be angry," Momma said. "I thought your friends might like the opportunity to wish you well before you jetted off across the ocean."

Well, it wasn't as if I hadn't been expecting it. Jake was just going to have to grin and bear it until it was time to leave for the airport. "How many folks did you invite?"

"Just a few," she said, and I could tell instantly that she was lying.

"Which means the entire town," Grace said happily, and then we all started laughing.

"Why not? Let's go," I said, and then I put my arm around my husband's. My, I liked the sound of that. "We might as well pretend it was our idea all along," I told him.

"It's going to be fine," Jake replied, much calmer than I'd expected.

"Seriously? You hate crowds, and you detest it when folks make a fuss over you. This is going to be both."

"True, but at least this way we can get all of the well wishes out of the way at once," he said. "That has to be better than being stopped on the street every other hour by folks for the next six months."

"Point taken, but this isn't going to keep folks from saying anything later."

"Let's just go and do our best to enjoy it," he said, surprising me for the first time as my husband. I had a feeling that it wouldn't be the last.

Later that evening, just after we'd boarded the plane to Paris, I turned to Jake and asked, "Are you still okay with the fact that Momma threw us a reception after our impromptu wedding?"

He laughed. "Ask me that again tomorrow in Paris. Fair warning. As soon as we settle into our seats, I plan on sleeping the entire way there."

"That sounds good to me," I said, echoing his sentiments. The airline had upgraded us to first class at the last moment when they found out we were newlyweds and realized that they had two seats available up front, and we were enjoying the luxury that entailed, though I realized that coming back in the economy class might be a little tough to take later.

For now, I was determined to enjoy it for all that it was worth.

Our honeymoon was even better than I'd dreamed it would be.

On our last day in Paris, we were eating chocolate croissants again from a bakery near our hotel as we strolled along the Seine. I looked over to find Jake grinning at me. "What is it? Do I have chocolate on my nose again?"

"Not yet, but I have high hopes for you. Has this been everything you dreamed it would be?"

"Paris, or being married to you?" I asked him with a smile of my own.

"I was talking about Paris, but I'll take an answer to either one."

I pulled him closer to me and said, "Both are beyond my wildest expectations."

"Are you sorry we have to go back home today?" he asked me as we passed another lamppost I'd grown to love so much. It was funny some of the things I'd come to enjoy.

"A part of me feels as though I could stay here forever," I said, "but I miss my shop. How about you? You don't have a job to go home to anymore."

"No, but I have a new bride, and that's good enough for me. It's going to be nice not having anything to do for awhile."

"How long do you think that might last?" I asked as I took the last bite of my croissant.

"You might be surprised. I'm looking forward to being a househusband."

"Good," I said, and then I glanced at my watch. "We'd better get back to the hotel. We're cutting it close as it is."

"I know you're right, but let's not rush this, okay? I just want to take it all in one last time." I wasn't sure what Jake had been expecting, but the city had really grown on him in our brief time there.

"We can always come back again, you know," I said, grinning.

"Maybe so, but this will be our only honeymoon," he answered a little wistfully.

"Who knew that under that tough-cop exterior lay the heart of a poet?"

"Shh, don't tell anybody," he said with a smile. "I don't want to jeopardize my tough-guy image."

The flight back was crowded, and there were no upgrades for us this time. Even with the proximity of so many other passengers on board, though, nothing could take the glow off our brand-new start as a married couple.

At least not until we saw my mother standing there waiting for us in the parking lot beside my Jeep.

Chapter 3

"Momma, what is it? Did something happen while we were gone?" I asked her as I rushed toward her. "Is it Phillip?"

"No, not really. Well, in a way, I suppose that you'd have to say yes. To be honest with you, at this point I'm not even sure what's happening," she said, clearly worried about something. It appeared as though she was fighting back tears, something very unlike my mother's usual behavior.

Jake touched her arm lightly. "Take a deep breath, Dot, and tell us what happened."

Momma did as he suggested, and after a moment, she seemed to be more collected than she'd been before. "It's Chief Tyler."

"What about him?" I asked. The man who'd taken over the April Springs police department hadn't made all that good an impression on me in the brief time that we'd known each other, and I had to wonder how he was involved in my stepfather's current situation. "Is he making life hard for Phillip now that your husband is officially retired?" It was hard for me to call the man by his given name, but now that he was retired, I didn't know what choice I had. I couldn't very well go on calling him Chief after he'd left the job.

"Suzanne, he's dead."

"What are you talking about? What happened?" Jake asked. The former state-police-investigator part of him was in full gear now. Though Jake had quit his job less than a few weeks before, I knew that it would take a great deal more time than that for him to get adjusted to civilian life, if he ever managed to do it at all.

"That's what's so puzzling. At first it appeared that he'd had a heart attack and passed away in his squad car, but it now seems that's not what happened at all."

"We'll get into that in a second. What I want to know is

who's in charge of the force right now?" Jake asked.

"Stephen Grant is the acting chief at the moment," Momma said. The young officer had been the interim boss at one point during the transition between Chief Martin and Chief Tyler, but it had been pretty clear that he wasn't ready for the job yet.

"Seriously?" Jake asked. "I didn't think he'd be put in charge again so quickly."

"What choice did George have?" she asked. "*Someone* had to take over." George Morris was the mayor of April Springs, and, as such, he had the authority to appoint a temporary chief if the current one was unable or unwilling to serve, something that seemed to be happening with increasing frequency lately in our little town.

"He could have always asked your husband to step back into the job," I suggested. While I'd never been Chief Martin's biggest fan, I truly believed that he was a decent law enforcement officer, all in all.

"That's where it gets tricky. Somehow Stephen Grant has it in his head that my husband might be involved in Alex Tyler's death."

I was about to ask how that was possible when Jake said, "I'm beginning to believe that this is too complicated to go over in an airport parking lot. Can we discuss this once we get back in town? You can follow us, or we'll follow you."

"Actually, I'll need a ride, since I don't have my car with me," Momma said. "Vince Jenkins was coming here anyway to fly to see his daughter, so I caught a ride with him. I thought it would be easier that way."

So much for easing into our new lives together on the drive home. What could I do, though? I couldn't exactly refuse my mother's request. Besides, we needed to be briefed on the situation before we stepped back into it.

"Then let's go," Jake said as he stowed our bags in the back of the Jeep.

"Would you like to drive?" I asked my new husband as I offered him the keys to my vehicle.

He managed a smile before he replied. "Thanks for offering, but it's your vehicle. I don't see any reason anything has to change just because we're married now."

I kissed him soundly, forgetting my mother for a moment. "Really, because I can think of at least a thing or two myself."

He smiled gently. "So can I, but let's focus on figuring out what happened while we were gone before we get into that."

Momma started to climb into the back when Jake said, "You take the passenger seat up front, Dot."

"Jake, I hate to do that to you. I know that you'll be cramped back there, and that's one of the best things about being so short. I fit just about anywhere."

"Nonsense. I'm not about to let my brand-new mother-in-law ride in back," he said as he leaned over and kissed her cheek. "I'll be fine."

After Momma got into the front seat beside me, I started the Jeep, and the three of us headed back to April Springs. Once we were out of the heavier traffic around the airport, I turned to Momma and said, "Now tell us everything."

"So much has happened that I honestly don't even know where to begin," my mother said.

"I've always felt that the beginning is as good a place to start as any," Jake said. "What happened after we left?"

Momma nodded. "That's right. I forgot that you both missed all of the fuss. It started just after you two took off for the airport."

"What happened?" I asked.

"Phillip and Alex got into a pretty heated argument," Momma said, "and I'm afraid that there were several witnesses to it."

"What could they possibly have had to argue about?" I asked her.

"Actually, it was you," Momma said.

"Me?" I was shocked that my name had even come up between the two law enforcement officers. "What did I have to do with it?"

"Phillip told Alex that he was being too hard on you and that he needed to take your input seriously. Alex told him that had been one of the main problems with the police department before, that amateurs were even allowed to have opinions in ongoing investigations. Things got rather heated, and I was afraid they might come to blows if it kept up. Stephen Grant had to step in between them, and I got Phillip out of there as quickly as I could manage it, but the argument certainly made an impression on everyone who was there."

"You still haven't told us how Tyler died," Jake said softly from the backseat. I'd moved my seat as far forward as I could to accommodate his long legs, but I was afraid that it hadn't been enough.

"As I said, at first everyone thought that it was a heart attack."

"He was so young, though," I said.

"I told you that was just at first. It was only after they checked more thoroughly that they found the poison in his system."

I had a sudden sinking feeling in my gut. "He wasn't found eating one of my donuts, was he?" My treats had been used as a murder weapon before, and I hoped and prayed that it hadn't happened again.

"There were no donuts in his system," Momma said, and I felt a sudden burst of relief.

It turned out to be short lived, though, as Momma continued, "The coffee he'd been drinking had been poisoned."

"Do I even have to ask where he got it?"

"The cup was from Donut Hearts," she admitted, and that's when I felt that sinking feeling all over again.

"This can't be happening," I said.

"Take it easy, Suzanne," Jake responded. "There's no reason to jump to any conclusions. There's no reason in the world anyone would think that Emma or Sharon could be involved in the murder."

"Actually, that's not entirely true," my mother said softly.

"What are you talking about?"

"Four hours before the new chief of police's body was found in his squad car, he had a pretty intense argument with Emma in the donut shop."

This was getting worse by the minute. "What were they fighting about?"

"Apparently he asked her out on a date, and when she refused him, he got a little belligerent. He threatened to shut the shop down for health code violations, and Emma dared him to go ahead and try. He took his coffee and stormed off, and a little later, Stephen Grant found his body in the squad car."

"That's just perfect," I said.

"Why do you think I met you at the airport?" my mother asked us. "You've got to do something."

My attention was on the road, so I didn't see who Momma was looking at, but I just assumed that it was me. "I'll do what I can," I said.

"Suzanne, I know that ordinarily you're quite capable of investigating murder on your own, but we have an expert at our disposal now." I saw her turn in her seat as she looked at my new husband. "Jake, what do you say? Will you do it?"

"Sorry. I'd love to help out, but I'm retired now," he said without much hesitation.

"Nobody's asking you to step in and be the police chief," Momma said, "but we all know that Stephen Grant is in over his head when it comes to murder."

"I can appreciate that, Dot, but remember, I don't have any standing in the case," Jake said.

"That's never stopped *me* before," I replied, glad at the prospect of Jake digging into this. Momma was right. While I'd had my share of success in the past solving a few murders, my husband had made a career of it. Only just recently retired from the state police as a special investigator, he would be perfect for the job. "Come on, it's fun from our side of the law."

"I wouldn't exactly call it fun," he said. "I like having the authority to compel folks to cooperate with my investigation."

"I've got that covered," Momma said with the hint of a smile.

"How did you manage that?" Jake asked her.

"I've already spoken to George. The mayor told me that all you need to do is say the word and you will be the April Springs Interim Special Investigator."

"That title didn't even exist yesterday, did it?" Jake asked skeptically.

"See, what did I tell you? You're an excellent detective," Momma said with a smile. "Jake, I wouldn't ask you to do this if it weren't important. It's killing Phillip to be suspected of murdering his successor, even if it is just idle gossip and Stephen Grant's speculation at this point. You've got to do something."

"Momma, even if your husband weren't a suspect, my employees and friends clearly are," I chimed in. "You need to do this for our family, Jake. We need you."

Jake was silent for some time, and I knew better than to speak while he was mulling something over. At one point I saw that Momma was about to say something, but I gave her a quick head shake, and she stifled it quickly. She might know a great many more things than I did, but no one in the world knew my husband as well as I did. That might not even be true, but I was going to assume that it was until I was proven wrong.

After what felt like an eternity, he finally spoke. "Let me get this straight. Stephen Grant will be in charge of the police force in general, correct?"

"Correct," Momma answered.

"And my duties will consist solely of finding Alex Tyler's killer."

"That's the way that I understand it," she replied.

"Fine, but I'm going to have to call my former boss before I take this on," Jake said.

I let my gaze shift from the road to my rearview mirror

momentarily. "Jake, you don't work for him anymore. You don't have to ask him permission for anything."

"That's where you're wrong, Suzanne. When it comes to foul play that involves a law enforcement officer, the state police investigative unit has priority and jurisdiction. I can work around the edges, but the heart of the case will be handled by one of my former coworkers. I just hope it's not Simpson."

I'd heard him mention the man's name a time or two in the past, and it had never been flattering. "Can you get him to assign one of your friends? How about Terry Hanlan?" I'd gotten to know Terry earlier, and it would be comforting to have him around.

"No, he's working a case in Franklin at the moment," Jake said.

"How could you possibly know that?" I asked him.

"I texted him the moment that your mother suggested that I investigate this murder," he answered.

"Wow, that was pretty slick. I didn't even realize you had your phone on you. I thought it was in your carry-on luggage."

"It was, but I slipped it out after we landed. Mandy's tied up, too. Don't worry. I have a few other friends on the force I can call."

I started to say something when I realized that Jake had meant right now. He started speaking, and it took a moment to realize that he wasn't talking to us. From what I heard of his side of the conversation, it wasn't going particularly well, and when he finished the call, I saw him scowling into the rearview mirror. "Well, that couldn't have gone worse."

"What happened? Was he unhappy about your new assignment?"

"Are you kidding me? He was ecstatic," Jake said.

"Why is that?" Momma asked.

"It's given him the perfect opportunity to stick it to me again for leaving."

"I'm not so sure that I like the sound of that," I said. The idea of someone bullying my husband didn't sit well with me at all. When I'd been married the first time to Max, I could remember bristling right alongside him over a bad review, but it had been nothing compared to the way that I was feeling now.

"It goes with the territory," Jake said. "The worst of it is that he's assigning Simpson to the case. He'll be in April Springs first thing tomorrow morning."

"Then we'd better get busy before he gets here," I said. "Momma, do me a favor and call Grace."

"I could always help you again this time," my mother said. "After all, this case has a direct link to my husband."

Momma and I had worked on one murder case before, but that had been under special circumstances. While we'd proved to be an effective team, I still preferred Grace's assistance over my mother's. I just didn't know how to tell her that without hurting her feelings.

Fortunately, Jake saved me from having to do it. "Dot, I'm sure that Suzanne appreciates your offer, but Phillip is the very reason that you shouldn't be involved in this investigation. It's bad enough that one of Suzanne's employees is a suspect, but the fact that one of the men who used to work under your husband now suspects that he might be involved in the murder just makes things even worse. The best thing for you to do in this case is to keep a low profile."

I could tell by the set of my mother's jaw that she wasn't particularly fond of the advice she was getting, but to her credit, she decided to take it anyway as she turned to me and said, "Fine, but if you and Grace need me, I'm never more than a phone call away."

"I know; I'm counting on it," I said. I made a note to myself to thank my husband for stepping in so graciously and saving me from having an awkward conversation with my mother.

Momma dialed Grace's number for me and put it on speaker. When my best friend answered, I said, "Hey, Grace, it's Suzanne."

"Hi! Welcome back! April Springs has been positively dead since you left." After a moment's hesitation, she added, "Given what just happened to our new head lawman, I should have probably come up with a better choice of words. But you haven't heard about that yet, have you? How was Paris?"

"It was everything I imagined, and more," I said, and before Grace could say anything else, I added, "We've already been brought up to speed. I'm on speaker right now. Momma met us at the airport, and the three of us are driving back to April Springs together."

"Wonderful," Grace said after a moment, no doubt reviewing our conversation to see if she'd said anything she might have to apologize for. When she concluded that she hadn't, she asked, "So, I have a hunch you're not calling to tell me that you're back. Are we investigating this murder?" Grace sounded almost eager as she said it, and I wondered yet again about how seriously she took our investigations. There was a part of me that was afraid she believed it was all some kind of game, even after we'd been faced with the prospect of dealing with cold-blooded killers in our past.

"Unofficially, as always. Jake is going to be the super special chief investigating deputy investigating it for the police department," I said.

Momma quickly corrected me. "Actually, his official title is April Springs interim special investigator."

"Woohoo. Aren't you special! I want the first business card you get after they print that title up," Grace said. "Congratulations, Jake. Or should I offer you my sympathies instead?"

"To be honest with you, it's still too soon to tell," Jake answered amiably enough.

"Okay. Keep me posted, though."

"Will do."

I decided that was enough banter for one telephone call. "Grace, I haven't asked anyone's permission to do this yet, but of course I'm planning to dig into this myself, so no one who knows me should be surprised by that fact." As I said it, I looked at Jake and smiled. He had the presence of mind to just smile back instead of arguing with me. "Are you free to lend me a hand?"

"I'm not, but I can be," she said. "I've got some vacation time I've been dying to burn. When do we get started?"

I glanced at the clock on the dash and saw that we were less than half an hour from getting home. "How about forty-five minutes? Does that give you enough time to get yourself free?"

"I'll make it work," she said. "Oh, and by the way, congratulations again. I'm truly happy you two found each other."

It was a nice sentiment of heartfelt feeling from her, a gesture that I greatly appreciated. "Thanks. See you soon."

"Bye," she said, and then she broke the connection.

I adjusted my rearview mirror so I could look squarely at Jake. "Well, it appears that our honeymoon is now officially over. Sorry about that."

"There's nothing to be sorry about," Jake said happily. "I never was all that interested in all of the hoopla leading up to us being together. The wedding and honeymoon were both nice, but it's the marriage itself that I've been looking forward to."

"I have to tell you, that's probably the nicest thing that anyone has ever said to me," I told him, and then remembered that my mother was sitting right beside me. "You know what I mean."

"Suzanne, I'm not about to argue with you. Who knew that he had that in him?"

"*I* knew," I said proudly.

"I'm still here, ladies, remember?"

"Oh, hush," Momma told Jake. "You should know that whenever people who care about you say nice things, your only job is to listen politely and say thank you when they're through."

Jake took a moment, and then he asked, "Are you

through?"

"For the moment," I replied.

"Then thank you," he answered.

Momma laughed loudly, and Jake and I joined in.

It might not be the best start a marriage ever had, but it was undeniably all ours.

Chapter 4

After we dropped Momma off at her place, I asked Jake, "Where to now? Should we head back to the cottage and unpack?"

"Why not?" Jake asked. "Suzanne, while we're there, there are a few things that we need to talk about."

"Have I done something bad already?" I asked him with a smile. "Wow, that didn't take long at all."

"We both know that you are just about perfect in my eyes," Jake replied with a grin.

"Right back at you, big guy. What exactly do we need to discuss, then?"

"What else is there at the moment? I'm talking about this case," he said.

"Excellent! Are you ready to share something with me already? Sweet! I knew there would be some perks being married to you, but I didn't expect them to come so quickly."

"Can we both be serious for a minute?" Jake asked rather soberly.

"Sorry. What do you want to talk about?"

"I'm running the official investigation, and you yourself urged me to take the job less than an hour ago, is that correct?"

"It is," I answered.

"And you don't want to make my life any harder than it has to be. Is that true as well?"

"Jake, I would never intentionally cause you problems. You should know that by now."

"I do," he said reassuringly as he patted my hand.

"It might be easier for both of us if you just cut to the chase and quit dancing around what's on your mind, okay?" I suggested.

"That's probably as good a plan as any," he said with a grin. "I understand why you have a vested interest in solving this case—two of them, actually—but I'm going to need my space on this one."

"Does that mean that you don't want *any* help from me?" I asked, trying to hide the hurt I felt. He had every right to make the request, but that didn't mean that I had to like it.

"All I'm saying is that you need to let me dig into this myself before you and Grace start ripping through my suspect list before I can get to them all."

"That sounds reasonable enough," I said, fighting to keep my voice level.

Evidently I failed.

"Suzanne, this isn't meant as a slight in any way, shape, or form."

"Why would I think that it was?" I asked him.

Jake was about to reply when his cell phone rang. "Saved by the ring," he said with a slight smile.

"Not saved, just delayed," I said with a grin to take the edge off my comment. I knew that we both had a lot of adjusting to do as newlyweds, and adding our sometimes conflicting investigations into the mix wouldn't do anything to make our new life together any easier.

As he spoke, I heard a stiffness suddenly enter his voice. His answers were nearly monosyllabic and gave little away, but I could tell that he was getting more upset by the minute. After he hung up, I asked, "Wow, who just poked you with a stick? Was that your old boss?"

"No, if anything, it was worse. It was Inspector Simpson, and he just read me the riot act."

"What can he do to you, honestly?" I asked. "It's not like you work for the state police anymore."

"If I did, at least I'd be able to fight back. As things stand, he is well within his rights to make certain demands, and I have no choice but to accept them all."

I hadn't met this guy and I already didn't like him. "What exactly did he say to you?"

"He told me that my investigation is confined to April Springs and April Springs alone. Anything out of town limits is forbidden."

"How can he do that?" I asked, the outrage clear in my voice. "It's not fair handcuffing you like that."

"Maybe not, but I'm not exactly sure that I have any choice. Remember what I said earlier?"

"About being there for me in sickness and in health?" I asked him with a gentle smile.

"After that. I'm talking about when I told you to hold off on your investigation."

"I'm not likely to forget that," I said.

"Well, you should. Disregard my earlier instructions. Leave April Springs to me. That still leaves an important area for you and Grace to explore."

I grinned at him. "We're going to cover what you can't. Is that it? You realize that there's a good chance that the root of Alex Tyler's murder is in Granite Meadows, not April Springs, don't you?"

"You really are becoming a first-rate detective; you know that, don't you?"

"Flattery will get you everywhere with me," I said with a grin.

"It's not flattery if I mean it," he said. "There are a few conditions I need to insist on before I set you two loose on the unsuspecting population of Granite Meadows, though."

"I'm listening."

"You have to do your best to fly under everybody's radar. You won't just be ducking Simpson. You'll also be trying to avoid antagonizing the police chief there as well. All the while, I need you to find out whatever you can about Alex Tyler and then report back to me."

I took a deep breath before I spoke again. "Let me get this straight. You want us to amass as many facts as we can, but then we have to turn it all over to you so you can be the detective. Is that about right?"

To his credit, Jake didn't answer immediately. Instead, he appeared to mull over my comment before he replied. After a few moments, he turned to me with a grin and said, "I'd say that sounds exactly like what I told you to do."

"You know in your heart that it's not going to work that way, don't you?"

Jake shrugged. "I can see where there might be difficulties. How about this? Try to keep from putting yourselves in jeopardy, but find out whatever you can, and we'll compare notes later."

"We can do that," I said, and then I kissed him quickly.

"What was that for?" he asked. "Not that I'm complaining."

"It's for being rational about this and understanding that you can't always have everything you want."

"No worries there," he said with a grin. "I know you pretty well, but even if I didn't, I'm pretty sure that I would have been able to figure that one out on my own."

We got back to the cottage and did a perfunctory job of unpacking, and then we started out on our separate ways, me in my Jeep and Jake in his old truck. There was no time for jet lag. We both had work to do. Before he could drive to the police station to be fully briefed, I leaned in through his window and said, "We really should find you a new truck to drive now that you're a civilian."

He put a hand over the dash before he answered. "Not so loud. She might hear you."

"You, sir, are too attached to a simple mode of transportation," I said.

"Said the pot to the kettle," he answered with a grin. "Tell me again how you feel about your Jeep."

"That's different," I said.

"How so?"

"It's simple. The Jeep is mine."

Jake just laughed. "I can't dispute the logic of that, so I won't even try."

"Good man. Stay in touch," I said as I got into my Jeep.

"That goes for you, too," he said, and I drove down the road to Grace's place to pick her up.

It was a short commute, yards instead of miles, but it was

far enough away for me to start getting antsy.

I wanted to get our own investigation underway, and I wanted to do it now.

"Welcome back," Grace said as she hugged me when I showed up on her doorstep. "I missed you."

"I missed you, too," I said as I handed her the bag I'd brought her all the way from Paris. "I'm still not sure about the choice of presents you requested."

"Let me see it," she said excitedly as her hand dove into the bag and pulled out a black beret with GRACE embroidered in large red letters. I thought it was going to look silly on her, but my best friend had such a style and polish about her that she actually pulled it off. "How do I look?" she asked, cocking it to one side.

"Spectacular. Now I'm wishing that I'd bought one for myself," I admitted.

"I'd let you borrow mine, but we don't want anyone mistaking us for each other," she said.

I looked at her trim figure and then contemplated mine for a moment. "No chance of that happening. Anyway, I'm glad you like it."

"Like it? I love it! Thank you, Suzanne."

"You are most welcome. Now, should we talk about the case?"

Grace slid the beret off and put it back into the bag. "That sounds good. How about some coffee while we brainstorm?"

"Do you happen to have any sweet tea? That's about the only thing I really missed while we were in Europe."

"You're in luck. I made a fresh batch this morning," Grace said.

After my first glass had been drained and then topped off again, Grace and I sat in the living room and talked about how we should approach the case.

"Where should we begin?" Grace asked. "I've picked up on a few things from Stephen, but he's been reticent to speak with me about the case much. My boyfriend can be pretty tightlipped when it comes to his job."

"That's perfectly understandable," I said. Besides, I already knew what Acting Chief Grant thought. There was potential for conflict between Grace and me. I realized that we were in a delicate area, and the less we touched upon it, the better, as far as I was concerned. "Well, here's what I've managed to learn so far," I said, and I started relaying everything that I'd learned from Momma on the drive back to April Springs.

"Can I ask you a question?" Grace asked after I was finished.

"Go ahead."

"If Jake has agreed to investigate this case, then what exactly are we doing? Isn't he likely to be offended by us digging into his own investigation?"

"I haven't told you that part yet. He's given us a green light to go to Granite Meadows and look around because one of his old adversaries from his state police days is now in charge of the investigation for his old boss."

"Why am I guessing that was done as a punitive measure?" Grace asked.

"I don't know, because you're smart, savvy, and you know people?" I asked.

"That must be it. So, what do we know about Alex's life in Granite Meadows?"

"Just that he was a cop there before he came here," I said. "Right now, the rest of the details are kind of sketchy."

"That's okay. We'll figure out how to fill them in. Let's go."

I had to laugh. "That's just one of the things I love about you, my friend."

"What's that?"

"Your complete and utter willingness to dive into the fire with me at a moment's notice."

"What are friends for?" she asked. "If they don't stand by your side when you need them, they aren't really friends in my book. You'd do the same for me, and you know it."

"You'd better believe it," I said as we got into the Jeep and starting driving toward Granite Meadows. I'd have to catch up with Emma and Sharon soon so we could figure out what we were going to do about Donut Hearts, but in the meantime, I had a murder to investigate with my best friend.

"Should we have packed our bags for an overnight stay?" Grace asked me.

"It's less than an hour from here. I think we'll be pretty safe commuting while we investigate."

"Sure, I get it."

"Get what?" I asked her.

"You've got a brand-new husband at home. Why on earth would you want to leave him so soon?"

"Jake has nothing to do with it," I said.

"Nothing?" As she asked it, there was a mischievous glint in her eye.

"Maybe not nothing, but that's not the main reason that I don't want to stay. I have a donut shop to run, remember?"

"You're kidding. You're actually going back to work tomorrow with everything going on?"

"Of course I am," I said. "I've been away too long as it is, and I miss it. Are you really all that surprised?"

"Now that I think about it, I realize that I shouldn't be," Grace replied. "There's a lot of you wrapped up into that place these days, isn't there?"

I thought about it for a moment before I answered, keeping my outward attention focused on the road in front of us. When I spoke again, I knew exactly what I wanted to say. "You know better than anyone but Momma that I never wanted to be a donutmaker when I was a little girl. To be honest with you, I kind of fell into it, seeing that the place was for sale at the only moment in my life when I could afford to buy it. Breaking up with Max was really painful, and I poured myself into Donut Hearts to get away from it. A funny thing happened, though. Instead of a way to hide from my life, the shop showed me a new one altogether. I can't ever imagine a time when I don't want to do it."

I saw Grace nodding out of the corner of my eye. "I was worried about you for a long time after Max," she said. "Everything you're saying about the donut shop is absolutely true."

I grinned at her. "Well then, if you knew the answer to the question already, why did you go ahead and ask it?"

"I knew. I just wasn't sure that *you* did," she said.

"Fair enough. We've got a little time; let's talk about how we're going to investigate Alex Tyler's former life in Granite Meadows."

"Well, the logical first step would be to go where he used to work," Grace answered. "That might be a little tough to do, though, since he was a cop."

"There are ways around that, but we need some information first. We don't even know where he used to live."

"Ah, that's something that I can help with," she said as she pulled out her cellphone.

"I forgot that you used that thing for more than making calls," I said with a laugh.

"You joke, but I can't imagine ever being without it. Now let's see. I've got my search engine up, so I'll type in Alex Tyler, Granite Meadows, North Carolina, police officer, home address. That should do it."

"That's a lot of information you're giving it," I said.

Grace said, "I've come to realize that the more specific the question, the more accurate the answer."

"That makes sense. What does it say?"

As she started scrolling through the listings, she finally said, "Bingo. We need to go to 3441 West Mulberry in Granite Meadows. That's where he used to live up until a few weeks ago."

"That's all well and good, but my Jeep doesn't have GPS."

"There's no need," Grace said as she shook her phone at me. "I've got it right here."

"Is there anything that it can't do?" I asked her.

"If they can figure out a way to have it rub my sore feet at night, I'd buy two of them."

"Doesn't the April Springs interim police chief do that for you already?"

She laughed. "Sometimes, but not as often as I'd like." After a moment's pause, she said, "The coordinates are now entered. All we have to do is follow directions and we'll be there."

"Do you trust it that much?"

"What makes you ask me that?" Grace inquired.

"I once read about a man who followed his GPS blindly and winded up driving into a river."

"Some common sense might be in order, too," Grace said, "but so far, it hasn't led me too far astray."

"Good, because we don't have a ton of time for any wild goose chases. What's our plan when we get to his old address?"

"We start knocking on doors and we talk to his neighbors. Hopefully we'll get someone nearby who's as nosy as Gabby Williams is in April Springs."

Gabby ran the gently used clothing store near the donut shop. It was called ReNEWed, and besides having some really nice things for sale, expensive clothes that had been barely worn, it was a hotbed for gossip. If Gabby didn't know it, some folks in town said that it really didn't happen.

"We should be so lucky," I said.

Grace laughed. "I never dreamed that anyone would say knowing Gabby was lucky."

"That's not true. She's been a friend to me since I've been at Donut Hearts," I said.

"Suzanne, are you actually defending her?"

I was as startled by the idea as Grace was. Gabby had been a thorn in my side on more than one occasion in the past, so why was I standing up for her now? I wasn't exactly sure. It just felt as though it was the right thing to do. "I guess I am, though I couldn't tell you exactly why," I answered lamely.

"Well, good for you," Grace said as we finally neared the sign welcoming us to Granite Meadows. "I heartily approve of loyalty, no matter what form it comes in." After a moment, she said, "Hey, my phone just died."

"Did you forget to charge the battery?" I asked her.

"It's got plenty of charge left. The signal just dropped out. We must be in a dead zone."

"Does that happen very often?" I asked her.

"More than I like. Hopefully we'll get it back soon."

"Otherwise we'll have to find his place the old-fashioned way," I said with a smile.

"What's that?"

"We stop at a gas station and ask directions."

Chapter 5

"Nobody's home," I said as I banged on the apartment door next to Alex's old place for the second time. Half a mile down the road, Grace had managed to pick up a signal again, and we were back on track. This was our fourth attempt to find someone home who might be able to help us, and it wasn't looking very promising so far. "Let's try another door a little farther down."

"I'd hoped that with him living in an apartment complex, it would be easy to interview his old neighbors, but I'm starting to lose faith that's going to happen."

As she spoke, I saw movement three doors down from where we stood, a fluttering window curtain that was quickly pulled shut when the person inside realized that I'd spotted them. "Hang on a second," I said as I casually walked toward the closest door to the movement. "We might have ourselves a live one."

Evidently Grace hadn't spotted the curtains. "Where are we going? We should try the closest places first, Suzanne."

"Trust me," I said as I rapped firmly on the door in question.

After a full thirty seconds, Grace and I were still standing there alone. Apparently my knocking had been to no avail.

"I'm telling you, it's a waste of time," Grace said.

I knocked again, winking at her in the process, and then I said loudly, "We're not selling anything. Someone you might know was murdered recently, and you could be able to help us find the killer." If that didn't get the attention of whoever was on the other side of that door, I didn't know what would. I could probably pull a fire alarm for the complex and wait to see who came out, but I didn't really want to do that. Maybe I'd call that Plan B.

After three seconds, I knocked again as I said, "We're not going anywhere, so you might as well speak with us. You'll feel better if you do. I promise."

Grace looked at me oddly for a moment, something that unfortunately wasn't all that unfamiliar to me.

This was getting ridiculous. I couldn't compel whoever was hiding behind that door to come out and speak with us. Maybe it was time to give up and move on to the next door. I was about to suggest that very thing to Grace when the door opened tentatively and a rather plain-looking gal in her late twenties poked her head out. "Who was murdered? It wasn't Alex Tyler, was it? I knew that something was wrong."

"I'm sorry to be the one to tell you, but yes, it was. Did you know him well?"

"He's really gone?" she asked, her voice barely above a whisper. The next thing I knew, she was collapsing.

I had two choices: catch her or let her fall.

I caught her.

"Are you okay?" I asked as I kept her from hitting the ground.

There was no reply.

Grace helped take some of the weight, but it was still an awkward burden. "Suzanne, let's get her inside."

"Should we just walk right into her apartment without being invited?" I asked, still surprised by the sudden turn of events.

"Well, I suppose we could just leave her spread out on the cement in front of her apartment," my best friend said with a chuckle. "It's up to you."

"You're right. Let's take her inside."

We carried the woman in and found a pretty unusual décor there. I'd been expecting a drab kind of interior, but the main living space looked as though a glitter bomb had gone off. There were snow globes of all shapes and sizes on just about every flat surface, and she'd even made her own glistening, giant snowflakes that hung from the ceiling and plastered the walls. Painted snowmen covered any free space available, and I felt myself shivering a little, and not because of the implied chill the scene evoked.

"Wow," Grace said as she stopped dead in her tracks and

looked around. "All I can say is wow."

"We can take in the winter wonderland after we get her on the couch," I said as I continued moving forward with our unconscious host.

"Right."

We quickly got her positioned on the couch, and I grabbed a blanket and put it over her. It was covered with wintry scenes as well, of course.

"Who does this?" Grace asked me, but I never got a chance to answer.

"I love winter," the woman said softly, her eyes slowly opening.

"Good. You're awake," I said as I got close to her. "Are you okay?"

"This isn't because of that kids' movie, is it?" Grace asked her.

"I've loved winter all of my life," she said. "Long before it became a trend, I have adored it."

"I'm sorry to be rude, but if that's true, why don't you live someplace farther north? I don't have to tell you that we rarely get snow around here at all."

The woman on the couch frowned before she spoke. I was going to have to get her name soon so I'd know what to call her. Otherwise I was going to start calling her Princess Snowflake or something ridiculous like that.

"I'd move in a heartbeat, but there's just one problem," she said as she struggled to sit up.

"What's that?" I asked as I helped her.

"I can't stand being cold."

I caught Grace fighting laughter, but she wasn't entirely successful at it. It wouldn't do to alienate this woman, but I was afraid that it was too late for that.

To my relief, she just smiled. "It's ironic, isn't it?" Then she studied us both briefly. "Who are you two, anyway?"

"I'm Suzanne, and that's Grace," I said. "In all of the excitement, we never caught your name."

"I'm Maisie Fleming," she said. "I don't know what

happened to me back there. I've never fainted before in my life."

"I'm sorry we gave you such a shock," I said. "We didn't realize that you and Alex were that close."

Maisie frowned, fighting back the tears before she spoke again. "We weren't; not really. I was on the edges of his life, never in the center of it."

"You would have liked that, though, wouldn't you?" Grace asked her softly.

I thought it might be a little too probing a question, downright inappropriate given that we'd just met this woman, but Maisie smiled as she shrugged slightly. "More than anything else in the world. Alex was wonderful."

I tried to imagine anyone referring to Alex Tyler as wonderful, but I couldn't visualize it. Maisie must have caught something in my gaze. "I realize that he wasn't perfect, not by any means, but that was one of the things that I saw in him. If he'd only had me by his side, I could have helped him become the man I knew that he could be someday."

"I've tried to fix a few men in my life before, too," Grace said in consolation as she sat down across from Maisie in a comfortable-looking chair. "It *never* worked out the way I hoped."

"This time it would have been different," she said stubbornly.

I had to end this line of conversation. "I'm sure you're right. Do you have any idea who might have wanted to hurt him?"

Maisie looked startled by the thought. "Do you think someone from Granite Meadows might have done it? How did he die, anyway? I just assumed that it was in the line of duty in his new job."

"As a matter of fact, somebody poisoned him," I said.

Maisie frowned for a moment as she took all of that in, and then she looked at both of us a little harder. "You two aren't with the police, are you? Neither one of you are wearing uniforms, and I haven't seen any badges since you've been here."

"They put the poison they used to kill him in a cup of coffee that I sell at my donut shop," I explained. "I wasn't there when it happened, but folks are wondering if my staff might have had something to do with it. I need to prove that they didn't."

"How can you be so sure that they weren't involved?" Maisie asked me pointedly.

"I'd stake my life on their innocence," I said. "Besides, if I thought they could be guilty, would I be in Granite Meadows trying to find the real killer?"

"You might if you were looking for a scapegoat to blame it all on," Maisie said. This woman was savvier than she'd first seemed.

"If I were going to do that," I said reasonably, "I would have stayed closer to home where I know everyone. Alex didn't make many friends in the short time he was in April Springs."

Defending the man even after his death, Maisie said, "He was hard to get to know at first, but once you did, you'd all have seen what a great guy he was."

"Maybe so, but we've heard rumors that there were folks here who never got to that point, either," Grace said. It wasn't hard to imagine that it was true, but we hadn't heard anything that supported it. My friend was taking a shot in the dark hoping to hit something that might eventually resemble a lead.

Maisie suddenly looked uncomfortable. "Sure, there were a few folks who had problems with Alex in town."

"Would you care to share any names with us?" I asked gently.

"I don't know if I should," she said after a moment's pause. "I don't want to point any fingers."

"Even if it might mean helping us catch his killer?" Grace asked.

That clearly made Maisie's mind up for her. "If you have

to start somewhere, it should be with Shannon Wright; that woman has to be high on your list of suspects. She was his ex-wife, and she hated him. I can tell you for a fact that woman's heart is made from ice, not stone, and if anybody wanted to see Alex dead, it had to be her."

"Does she still happen to live in town?" I asked.

"She does."

After Maisie provided the address, Grace asked, "Who else should we speak with?"

The floodgates were clearly now open, and Maisie seemed almost eager to share her list of suspects with her. "To be honest with you, I never really cared much for Alex's partner. He and Alex had a pretty nasty argument when Alex took the job in April Springs. Someone actually had to call the police! Can you imagine? The chief himself broke it up, and believe me, Robert Willson wouldn't leave his desk chair for anything short of an all-out emergency."

"Anyone else we should speak with?" I asked her.

"Well, Deke Marsh has been hanging around Alex a lot lately, and they weren't exactly best friends, if you know what I mean."

"What's this Deke's story?" Grace asked.

"Alex arrested him recently, but he got out on a technicality last month. Since he's been released, I've seen him hanging around the building watching Alex come and go. He's somebody you should talk to, if you're brave enough. I cross the street whenever I see him, but that's just me."

"Is there anyone else you can think of?" I asked her.

"No, not that I know of." Maisie stood, letting the blanket fall back to the couch. "I'm feeling much better now. Thanks for helping me inside." As she spoke, she kept walking us toward the front door of her apartment.

"We're truly sorry for your loss," I said, trying to delay our exit in the hopes of getting something else out of her.

"As I said before, ultimately, we weren't all that close. Most of our relationship took place in my imagination. It's sad; that's all."

We were at the door now, and Grace and I really had no choice but to leave. I snatched a business card from my wallet and handed it to her. It was from the donut shop, one of a gift of a hundred from my mother last Christmas. I still had ninety-seven left. "If you think of anything or anyone else we should consider, don't hesitate to call."

"I will," she said, and then the door closed.

I glanced at Grace, who grinned back at me, and then she started singing, "Let it snow, let it snow, let it snow."

"Not today, though," I said. "We have some suspects to track down and interview."

"Then let's get to it, shall we? Who should be first on our list?"

After a moment's thought, I said, "We should absolutely go after the civilians first. I've got a hunch that the cops are going to be a lot harder to crack. Besides, Jake told me that we should keep as low a profile as possible for as long as we can."

"That sounds like a plan to me, then. Let's start with Shannon. Ex-wives are my specialty, you know."

As I started driving to the address Maisie had given us, I said, "I'm glad you feel that way, because I always dread talking to them, myself," I said.

"Why on earth should you? Who couldn't love a bitter ex that can't wait to dish dirt on their former love?"

"I don't know. It's all kind of depressing to me," I said.

"That's because you're a newlywed," Grace said with a grin. "You want the entire world to be full of love and rainbows right now, and why shouldn't you? You're still on your honeymoon, after all."

"Grace, please tell me that you're not really as cynical as you sounded just then."

"I'm not," she replied. "I just haven't had the luck with men that you've had."

I decided not to remind her of my disastrous marriage to Max. "Things are looking up with Stephen, aren't they?" I asked as I pulled into the complex where Shannon lived.

"They are indeed, even if his new job is making it harder between us. He's under a lot of stress right now, and there doesn't seem to be anything I can do to help him. Do you have any advice?"

I laughed. "I learned a long time ago not to give anyone advice when it comes to their love lives. That's a road full of potholes and speed bumps."

Grace laughed right along with me. "Point taken."

"That being said," I added, "all you can really do is just be there for him." I glanced over and saw that Grace was grinning at me. "What's so funny about that?"

"The advice is solid enough," she said as we got out of my Jeep. "You just contradicted yourself by giving it."

"What can I say? I'm allowed to break my own rules every now and then, especially when it comes to you."

"Thanks for making the exception," she said. "We should keep in mind that Shannon might not be entirely sympathetic to our cause of finding her ex's killer, so she might not be entirely cooperative. Any suggestions on how we handle it if she tries to shut us down?"

"If she won't help us willingly, we really don't have any choice but to imply that the police might be looking at her if we can't give them something."

"I like it. There's nothing like the fear of reprisal to get someone to spill their secrets."

"It's just a backup plan, though," I reminded her.

"Got it. Let's do this."

As I reached out to ring Shannon's apartment bell, I couldn't help wondering again if Grace wasn't enjoying this a little too much. I often worried that she didn't take what we did seriously enough. I supposed that it was easy to forget that we were dealing with potential killers during our interviews, but I felt the need to remind her every so often. She enjoyed the cat-and-mouse nature of the questioning and then the digging, and maybe that was what made her so good at it. I wasn't always willing to push our suspects as much as she did. That was probably what made us such a good team.

Grace was our brashness, while I tried to be more methodical in our approaches.

At least it had worked for us so far.

Chapter 6

When Shannon Wright opened the door to her apartment, it was as though she were making a grand entrance into a hotel ballroom. She was lovely—there was no denying it—but in a shallow, superficial way. Underneath her expression, it was clear to me that there was nothing but ice. I had to admit that her dress was exquisite, showing off her rather spectacular figure to its greatest advantage, and her makeup had been expertly applied. All in all, she presented herself as a brightly wrapped package, but I had to wonder if there was anything of substance inside.

"Hello?" she asked. "May I help you?"

"We're hear to discuss Alex Tyler's murder with you," Grace said right out of the gate. There was no hesitation in her voice as she spoke or any sign that she didn't have complete conviction that Shannon would talk to us.

"Murder? I understood that it was a heart attack," Shannon said with just the slightest hesitation in her voice.

"That's what they thought at first, but after the medical examiner's report, they know that he was poisoned," I offered.

Alex Tyler's ex shuddered slightly. "Horrid. That's just horrid. I'm afraid I don't know what it has to do with me, though."

"Once upon a time you were married to the man, weren't you?" Grace asked her.

"It felt as though it was a lifetime ago. I hadn't seen him in ages."

"When exactly might that have been?" I asked her.

It was worth a shot, but after a moment, it was clear that there was no way she was going to answer that without asking a question of her own first. "I'm sorry, but we haven't been introduced."

"I'm Suzanne Hart, and this is Grace Gauge. We're working on the investigation."

Shannon seemed startled by my statement, as well she might be, since we had no official status. "Not with the Granite Meadows police. I know that much."

"The truth is that right now we're collecting information for the special investigator in April Springs," Grace said. That was twelve shades from the truth since Jake had told me that he couldn't officially sanction what we were doing, and I was about to correct it when I was interrupted.

"I can't help you. I don't know anything about it," Shannon said, and then she started to close the door in our faces.

"You know, it won't look good that you aren't cooperating," Grace said solemnly.

"I can assure you that I don't care how it looks," Shannon retorted.

"So, for the record, you have opted not to cooperate; is that correct?" I asked her.

That brought a frown to her lips. "For what it's worth, Alex was a bore while we were married, and nothing changed afterwards. If you need someone to speak with about his most recent activities, you should really talk to Maisie Fleming."

That caught me by surprise. "Maisie? Why should we speak with her?"

Shannon scowled as she explained, "She always kept quite a pretty close eye on my former husband. As a matter of fact, she confronted me soon after our divorce, telling me that I'd never deserved him. As if she did. The woman was obsessed with Alex, and I'm sure that her ardor hadn't receded over the months since we split."

"It was just a harmless crush, though, wasn't it?" I asked, trying to picture Maisie as a stalker.

"I chose the word 'obsessed' most carefully. Don't be taken in by her harmless demeanor. The woman is more dangerous than she appears to be. Now if you'll excuse me, I have plans."

I wasn't sure that she really did, but if something *had* been scheduled, I doubted that it would include us.

Once we were dismissed, I turned to Grace as we walked back to my Jeep. "Do you believe anything she said about Maisie?"

"I kind of do," Grace said. "You saw Maisie's place. What kind of woman around our age turns her entire apartment into a winter wonderland? It's clear that she's easily obsessed by things. How hard is it to make the jump to believing that she was obsessed with Alex, too?"

"I hadn't thought of it that way," I said. "That's worth some consideration."

"Save your thinking for the drive back home," Grace said. "We have a known criminal to interview next."

"Where do you suppose we'll find Deke Marsh?" I asked.

"I'm guessing the closest bar might not be a bad place to start," Grace replied.

"It's as good a guess as any," I answered.

We found a place on the edge of town, and Grace and I walked in together. It was dark, and music blared from the jukebox as we approached the bartender. There were maybe half a dozen men and women there, but nobody even looked up from their drinks as we approached him.

"We're looking for Deke Marsh," I said.

"Sorry, never heard of him," the bartender answered curtly as he went back to polishing the counter in front of him.

"Are you sure?" Grace asked, and I saw her waving a twenty-dollar bill in the air.

"Unless you want to use that to buy yourself a drink, you can put it away. Twenty bucks isn't going to change my answer."

Grace was unfazed by his response. "How about a hundred?"

I saw the bartender glance quickly toward one of the booths, and then he turned back to us. "Nope, not a hundred, either."

"Thank you for your time," I said as I tugged on Grace's arm.

"Suzanne, I'm not finished with him," she protested as I pulled her back toward the door.

"You did all that you needed to do," I whispered as we walked out together. Once we were out the door, I pulled Grace off to one side where we weren't immediately visible from the exit.

"What are we doing now?" Grace asked me plaintively.

"We're waiting."

We stood there a full thirty seconds before anything happened, though it felt much longer to me. I could see that Grace was about to speak as the door opened, so I shushed her. A man stepped outside, scanned the parking lot, and then began exploring his more immediate vicinity.

Evidently we hadn't hidden as well as I'd hoped, because he started walking toward us the instant he saw us. "That was pretty slick, ladies," he said as he approached.

"Deke Marsh, I presume?" I asked as I took a step forward to meet him.

"That depends. Who's asking?"

"We're here looking into Alex Tyler's murder," I answered.

The man looked genuinely surprised by the statement. "Murder? I heard it was a heart attack."

"As a matter of fact, it was poison," I said.

The former convict shook his head in obvious disgust. "Poison is for cowards. Even Tyler deserved better than that."

"We heard that you'd been stalking him since you got out," I said. Grace was leaving this one up to me. I wasn't sure if that was a good thing or not.

"Somebody's been lying to you," he said.

"Our source is pretty credible," I answered, though I wasn't sure anymore if that was actually true. Shannon had seeded some doubt in my mind about Maisie's trustworthiness, but I didn't need to tell Deke Marsh that.

"Maybe so, but they got this one wrong."

"Are you saying that you didn't resent being arrested and

thrown in prison?" Grace asked, finally deciding that it was time to speak up.

"First of all, it was jail, not prison."

"What's the difference?" Grace asked.

Deke Marsh laughed. "I've done time in both, and believe me, there's a difference."

"What's the second point?" I asked him.

"I served a month before I got out because of the DA's screw-up. I never claimed that I didn't do it. Was I happy that good old Alex decided to reform and arrest me? Not so much. I admit that I had a score to settle with him, but somebody took care of him before I got my chance."

"Reform? What is that supposed to mean?" I asked him. The cop I'd known had been by the book, to the letter, and though I hadn't liked him, I couldn't imagine him doing anything corrupt.

"When he was here, he took payoffs just like some of his other pals on the force, and then all of a sudden he started turning them down and getting all righteous about it. That made a lot of folks upset with him, on both sides of the law."

"You're trying to get us to believe that the police force in Granite Meadows all take bribes?"

"Not all of them, just a few," he said with a shrug. "A bought cop should stay bought, if you ask me."

"Why should we believe you?" Grace asked him.

"Ladies, I don't give a flip what you believe. Now if you'll excuse me, I have things that need to be taken care of. Good night."

After he drove away in a late-model sedan, I asked Grace, "Did you notice that he didn't ask us who we were or why we were asking him questions about Alex?"

"I noticed," Grace said. "Do you believe anything he just told us?"

"What, about the cops here being dirty? I don't know. I'll tell you one thing: I can't imagine it ever happening in April Springs."

"This isn't April Springs, though, is it?" Grace asked me.

"We need to talk to Jake about this before we do anything else," I said. "He'll know how we should handle it."

"Do we really need to do that before we talk to Alex's ex-partner on the force?"

"We do," I said. "We're heading back to April Springs right now. Is that okay with you?"

"I'm fine with it. It will give me a chance to knock out some paperwork when we get back. I may be on vacation, but some of that work has to be done regardless."

"Then we'll take this back up tomorrow after I close the donut shop for the day and have a chance to talk to Jake about what we've discovered so far."

"I'll be ready," Grace said. "Are you absolutely sure that you want to go back to the donut shop so soon after your honeymoon? I'll bet Emma and Sharon wouldn't mind staying on a few more days."

"Are you kidding? I can't wait to get back to work. I've really missed getting my hands in the batter and the dough."

"You've really found your perfect niche, haven't you?"

"I have," I admitted. "Face it; you love what you do, too."

"Sure, but look at how much I make. Add the fact that I can pretty much name my own hours most days, and what's not to love?"

"I feel the same way about running Donut Hearts," I said.

"Then we're both exactly where we belong."

After dropping Grace off at her place, I headed the last few dozen feet down the road to the cottage that I was now sharing with Jake. I knew that the odds weren't good that he'd be there now. After all, he was running his own investigation.

I wasn't expecting to find anyone else there, though.

Chapter 7

"Emma, Sharon, what are you two doing here?" I asked as I approached my assistant and her mother, who were standing on my front porch. "Were we supposed to meet up this evening?"

"No, but we took a chance that you'd be here," Emma said. "When we saw that you weren't, we were going to leave you a note," she said as she offered me a folded sheet of paper.

"Can't you just tell me what it says, or do I really need to read it?" I asked with a grin.

"Sorry," Emma said as she tucked the note into the front pocket of her jeans. "It's about what happened while you were gone."

"Why don't you both come on in and we can talk about it," I said as I unlocked the front door and opened it. It was chilly in the cottage, but I knew how to fix that. "Let me light a fire and make us some coffee."

"Don't go to any trouble on our account. We won't be here that long," Sharon said.

"Well, I'm cold, so I think I'll do it anyway," I said as I lit the fire I'd laid in the grate before Jake and I had left for our honeymoon. It was amazing to me just how much had changed in such a short period of time.

As the kindling took to the flame, I headed for the kitchen and flipped on the coffeepot. "That's going to take a few minutes. Now, tell me all about what happened. I heard Alex Tyler asked you out on a date. You usually don't argue with the men you turn down, Emma."

"I knew it wouldn't take long before everybody in town found out," my assistant said, clearly on the verge of tears.

"Take a deep breath, sweetie," Sharon said in that soothing, calm voice that all mothers seemed to acquire naturally. "Would you like me to tell it?"

"No, thanks. I can handle it." After expelling a deep breath, Emma continued. "Alex came by and started flirting with me. The shop was empty, so I guess he thought that was his opportunity. Boy, was he ever wrong. I didn't lead him on, though; I swear it."

"I believe you," I said as I reached out and patted her hand. "Go on."

"Well, he clearly wasn't used to being rejected. The more I refused his advances, the more belligerent he became."

"And that's when I came out front," Sharon added. "I heard Emma raising her voice, so I knew that something was going on. When I got there, Alex was trying to get behind the counter to get closer to her."

"What did you do?" I asked.

"Well, I *thought* about hitting him with a tray of donuts," Sharon said with a wry grin, "but I ended up scolding him instead, and that seemed to work well enough. Emma told him again that she wasn't interested in him, so he finally left."

"I'm curious about something. How did everyone in town find out about what happened if the shop was empty at the time?"

"Evidently Gabby Williams was standing just outside the front door when it happened," Emma said grimly. "She must have heard it all, and after that, it was too late to stop her."

"Believe me, I know what that's like," I said. Though I'd told Grace that Gabby and I were friends, sometimes the woman had the oddest way of showing it. "I've got a question for you. Did he happen to buy a cup of coffee while he was here?"

"No, he didn't. Why?"

"Haven't you heard? He was poisoned, and they found traces of what killed him in one of our cups from Donut Hearts."

"But that's impossible," Emma cried. "I never sold him a cup."

"Then he must have gotten it from someone else," I said with a frown. "Emma, could you make a list of everyone you sold a cup of coffee to on the day of the murder?"

My assistant frowned before she answered. "It might not be complete, but I should be able to come pretty close. Why, is it important?"

"Sweetie, she wants to know who might have bought one and poisoned it before giving it to the new police chief," Sharon explained, and then she looked at me. "Is that right?"

"It is," I said.

"Suzanne, do you have some paper and a pen I can borrow? I'll make the list for you right now."

I grabbed the pen and pad I kept by the landline phone for messages and handed them to her. "Thanks. It might help."

"I'll do whatever I can," Emma said, and then she started writing down names.

"What does your husband make of all of this?" I asked Sharon as Emma compiled her list.

"You know Ray. He sees conspiracies everywhere. You wouldn't believe some of the theories he's been playing with since this happened."

"Sadly, I would," I said.

"Suzanne, I know you two don't get along, but you should know that Ray's heart is in the right place."

"I'll take your word for it," I replied, "but only because you married him, and he helped raise such an excellent person."

"Hey, I can hear you," Emma said as she looked up with a grin.

"Why would I not want you to hear what I just said?" I answered with a smile of my own.

After another full minute, Emma handed me the pad and pen. "That's all I could remember. There were a few folks who came by that day that I didn't recognize."

"Could you describe any of them to me?" I asked as I took the pad from her and tore off the sheet with her list.

"Let me think about it a second," Emma said with a frown. "Let's see. There was a heavyset man in his fifties. I remember him because he was wearing a bowtie. You don't see many of those these days."

I made a mental note of her description in case he turned up later in the case. "Who else?"

"We had a plain woman in her late twenties/early thirties come by for a cup. She was memorable because of what she ordered more than because of how she looked."

"What did she get?"

"Mom and I made some snowman donuts while you were gone. I wasn't sure how they looked after they'd been in the fryer, but this woman seemed obsessed with them. She kept going on and on about how lovely anything dealing with snow was. It was kind of weird, actually."

That had to be Maisie! What had she been doing in April Springs? Was she stalking Alex in his new home, or was there some other, darker reason for her visit?

"Anyone else?" I asked.

"Yes. We had the oddest couple come in. He was barely five feet tall, and she was well over six feet. He kept looking up at her with such devotion that I envied her."

"Got it. Who else?"

"There was one woman who was rather striking. She sneered at our donuts and insisted on black coffee. She was quite elegant, but there was something about the way she acted, as though she were better than everyone else around her, you know? When I handed her the change from her drink, she visibly shuddered when my hand touched hers."

Could that have been Shannon? It certainly sounded like her. I wished that Grace and I had taken photos of the folks we'd talked to earlier. They would have come in handy about now.

"Is that it?"

Grace frowned. "That's all that I can think of. Sorry. I'm sure there were a few others, but I can't for the life of me remember what they looked like. You know how it gets around here sometimes."

"You did fine. If you remember anyone else later, let me know, okay? It could be important."

"I'll try my best," she said. "Suzanne, would you like to take a few more days off? It's okay with us if you do."

"Why does everyone keep asking me that? To tell you the truth, I can't wait to get back to work."

"That's perfectly fine with us," Sharon said. "We just wanted to make the offer."

"Sharon, I can't thank you enough for stepping in for me on such short notice. I'll have your pay ready tomorrow by eleven."

"There's no hurry," she said.

"So, which trip are you saving for next?" Sharon and one of her old girlfriends from high school loved to travel, and her working time at the donut shop helped finance her trips. Getting Ray out of town was next to impossible, but Sharon never seemed all that upset about it. Who could blame her? If I were married to Ray Blake, I'd take every trip that I could afford, too.

"We're thinking of touring rural Italy this time," she said rather wistfully. "Or perhaps Scotland. We're not sure yet."

"Well, wherever you end up, I'm sure that it will be lovely," I said. "Shall I get us some coffee? It's bound to be ready by now."

"Thank you, but I must be going," Sharon said. "Emma, you're free to stay behind if you'd like."

"I appreciate the offer, but I think I'll tag along with you." As I stood and showed them out, Emma hugged me. "I'm glad to have you back, Suzanne."

"Even if it means that you're back on dish duty?" I asked her with a laugh.

"You know me. I'm always ready for some solitude, some suds, and some songs," she said, grinning.

"Then you'll get more than your share of all three tomorrow," I promised.

I just hoped that I could follow through on it. When I was in the midst of a murder investigation, I wasn't always the most present owner of my donut shop, but I tried my best to be there when the doors of Donut Hearts were open.

"See you in the morning," Emma said, and she and her mother headed for the door.

"Would you like to sleep in?"

"Do you mean all day?" she asked me.

"I was thinking more like an extra hour," I replied.

"Sold," she said. "See you then."

After they were gone, I decided to have that cup of coffee and curl up on the sofa by the fire. Paris had been lovely, but in the end, there was no place like home, and I had someone to share it with now that I loved more than anyone else in the world.

Ten minutes later, I glanced at the clock and saw that it was nearing time to eat. Was there a chance that Jake would make it back to join me? There was only one way to find out.

I grabbed my cellphone and called him.

"Hey, I miss you," I said when he answered, though I hadn't known that I was going to say that until I'd blurted it out.

"I miss you, too. Paris seems pretty far away right now, doesn't it?"

"We could always go back," I said with a grin.

"We could, but it wouldn't be the same," Jake replied.

"Why, because I wouldn't have my inheritance from my aunt to blow on the trip?" I asked him with a laugh.

"No, it's because it wouldn't be our honeymoon the next time," Jake said simply.

It was quite a romantic thing to say, even if it had been delivered matter-of-factly.

"Agreed. Is there any chance you'll make it back to the cottage for dinner? I'm here, and I'm getting a little hungry."

"Are you and Grace back in town already? How did it go in Granite Meadows?"

"It's too involved to go into over the phone," I said. "What about dinner?"

"I'm starving," he admitted. "Whatever leftovers you can find in the fridge will be good enough for me. I'm not all that picky."

"You know that I can't resist a man who has a low bar," I

said. "Let me see what I can whip up."

"See you soon," he said, and then, almost as an afterthought, he added, "Love you."

"Love you, too," I said, warm from the recitation.

I poked my head into the fridge and was happy to find that Momma had used her key while we'd been gone, leaving us her famous ground chicken casserole. I heated the oven and popped it in, and just as the timer went off signaling that it was ready to eat, Jake walked in.

"Perfect timing," I said as I kissed my new husband.

"Sometimes it's better to be lucky than good," he said, and then he took a deep breath and smiled. "Did your mother stop by?"

"Not recently. She must have loaded our fridge while we were gone."

"It appears that I've won the lottery for mothers-in-law," Jake said with a smile, and then he wrapped me up in his arms. "I didn't do too badly in the wife one, either."

"Flattery will get you everywhere," I said with a grin, and then I pulled dinner out of the oven and served it. "Should we talk about the case while we eat, or would you rather postpone it until later?"

"It's your call," Jake said. We were still trying to find our way as a married couple, and because of that, we were both tiptoeing around each other as though we were a pair of delicate flowers.

"Let's go on and share," I said. "Do you want to go first, or should I?"

"You go. That way I can start eating right away," he replied happily.

I took a bite, and then I began to bring him up to speed on what I'd been up to since I'd seen him last. After I'd clued him in on our conversations with Maisie, Shannon, and Deke, he whistled softly. "You accomplished quite a bit before you came back home."

"Not as much as we'd hoped. Jake, I might need your help interviewing Craig Durant and Chief Willson."

"Do you think the police chief might have had something to do with what happened to Alex?"

"Not really, but he might know someone who could have had a grudge against Alex. After all, wouldn't his boss know something like that?"

"Not necessarily. You'd be surprised by just how much my former supervisor was in the dark about what I did on a daily basis. He always claimed it was intentional so he wouldn't be involved directly in my investigations in order to serve as a buffer if I ever got into trouble, but I have a hunch it was out of sheer laziness."

"Will you speak with the two officers in Granite Meadows with us?"

Jake frowned a moment before he spoke. "Suzanne, we're dancing near that line again."

"Which line is that?"

"The one where I act in my official capacity in April Springs while you and Grace work behind the scenes. George hired me to investigate the murder, but my old nemesis from the state police is keeping a pretty close eye on me. If Simpson sees something that he doesn't like, he can strong-arm George into shutting me down completely, and neither one of us wants that, do we?"

"No, having you on the inside is our best chance of solving this murder," I said. "I suppose Grace and I will have to tackle those two ourselves."

"Give me some time to think about it before you do anything else," Jake said, and I knew that he'd be playing with possible ways to help me throughout the rest of the evening. It was wonderful having him in my corner, and I knew better than to rush him.

"Now, tell me about your day," I said as I took a bite. No surprise, it was absolutely delicious. But then what did I expect from my mother?

"Well, I spent most of it butting heads with Manfred Simpson," he said as he frowned. "He came a day early! I thought I'd at least have until tomorrow morning, but he thought he'd get a jump on things. He set up shop in the chief's old office; can you imagine that? Poor Grant has to run the department from his old desk on the floor. I have to tell you, it wasn't all that pleasant being on the other end of the conversation with Simpson this afternoon. I was above him in seniority when I was with the state police, but he didn't hesitate to let me know that I was under his thumb now."

"Is his first name really Manfred? Why on earth doesn't the man have a nickname? Or does he actually like it?"

"It's a point of pride with him. His great-grandfather was named Manfred, and evidently the man was some kind of hero. Some of the guys tried calling him Manny once, but he got so angry that no one ever did it again, at least not to his face. Simpson just seemed easier after that, though we called him a lot worse than Manny behind his back."

"So now he's getting even with you," I said.

"Don't worry about it. I can handle him. The problem is that since he's restricted me to April Springs, I can't contact anyone from Granite Meadows directly. That's why I'm not sure that I can help you and Grace with your investigation."

"How does he expect you to solve Alex Tyler's murder if he's not willing to let you investigate wherever your leads take you?"

"Are you kidding? He'd love nothing more than me failing," Jake said. "If he can solve the case himself, I'd never hear the end of it."

"It's not like you two still work together," I said.

"Doesn't matter. He's a small and petty man. He'll find a way to stick it to me every chance he gets."

I reached across the table and patted his hand. "Then we'll just have to solve the murder ourselves."

"Thanks, Suzanne. It's good to have you on my side."

It was a big admission for him to make, especially given how he'd once felt about my amateur sleuthing. Over the last several months, he'd been starting to see the value I brought to the table with my detective work, but it was still nice hearing it from him.

Once we finished with the main course, Jake pushed his plate away. "That was excellent. I'm stuffed."

"Does that mean that you don't have any room for dessert at all?" I asked him teasingly.

"Well, I might have a bite or two of whatever we've got. Otherwise it would just be rude to your mother after she went to all of the trouble of making us something. What are we having?"

I laughed as I stood. "I have no idea if she brought us any treats or not, but I'll look."

"But you offered," he said, sounding a little hurt.

"I just wanted to see what you'd say," I replied.

"Suzanne, that's just cruel. Never offer a man dessert when there isn't any."

His tone was more serious than the conversation merited, and I could see that he wasn't entirely kidding. "Point taken. I'm sorry. If there isn't anything available, I'll whip something up."

"No need to do that. Apology accepted." Thankfully, that had mollified him, but I still kept my fingers crossed as I dove back into the fridge hoping that there was a treat there I could offer Jake.

Unfortunately, there was not.

Now I was in serious trouble.

Chapter 8

I was about to confess to Jake that we didn't have dessert when the doorbell rang. "Were you expecting someone?" I asked him as I moved to answer it.

"No, how about you?"

"Not a soul, but we'll know soon enough, won't we?"

I opened the door and found my mother standing on the front porch, a crumb-topped apple pie held reverently in her hands. "Am I interrupting anything?" she asked as she thrust the pie forward. "I thought you might like dessert."

"Is that pie I smell?" Jake asked from behind me. I hadn't even heard him leave the kitchen table.

"I thought you were full," I reminded him as I stepped aside and Momma came in.

"That was the main course. There's always room for some of your mother's pie." He looked at Momma and grinned. "Dot, you're bound and determined to keep me from ever making a mother-in-law joke, aren't you?"

"Feel free to tease me all you'd like to," Momma said with a warm smile that suddenly narrowed. "Just be aware that there's a point where it steps over the line. Cross that, and that's when the pies stop coming."

"Believe me, I won't even get close to it," he said as he kissed her cheek.

"I know you won't," Momma said as she put the pie down on the dining room table. "I see you found the ground chicken casserole I left you," she said with obvious approval.

"Thanks for doing that, Momma," I said as I kissed her cheek as well. "It was wonderful finding it there after our long trip."

"I was hoping that you'd enjoy it." Her smile faded as she added, "Actually, I had another reason to come by besides my pie delivery."

Jake piped in, "That's reason enough on its own any time, Dot. I'm going to get three plates. Are there any objections?"

"I made another pie just like this one for Phillip, so you two can share this one," Momma said.

"If you're sure," he said with a wicked grin. The man certainly loved pie, especially the treats my mother made. Mine were good enough, but I'd have to take another lesson from Momma to bring my skills closer to her level.

"I'm positive. It does me a world of good seeing how much you enjoy my little offerings," Momma said.

"Then far be it from me to disappoint you," Jake said as he stepped out of the dining room and into the kitchen to retrieve two plates, two forks, and a knife.

"You said earlier that there was another reason you came by?" I reminded Momma once Jake was out of the room.

"Yes. I need to give you this, Suzanne," she said as she reached into her pocket and pulled out two keys on a small silver ring.

I was about to ask what locks the keys worked for when I realized that they were both to the cottage. "Momma, this place is yours. You should always have your own set of keys."

"That's the second order of business," my mother said as she reached into another pocket and pulled out a sheaf of papers.

"I don't understand," I said as I took them from her.

"It's all fairly self-explanatory. This cottage is my wedding present to the two of you."

"Jake, get in here right now," I called out.

There must have been something in my tone of voice, because he came immediately, even without the plates and utensils. "What is it? What's wrong?"

"Momma's trying to give us this cottage," I said, barely able to get the words out.

"That's too generous of you, Dot," Jake said in protest.

"Nonsense. Besides Phillip, you two are all that's left of my immediate family. I want you to have it."

"But this place has always belonged to you," I protested.

"We both know that's not true. When your father and I

married, his mother signed the deed to this cottage over to us, and now it's your turn. Besides, I already have a place to live."

"I'm not trying to talk you out of letting us live here, but that doesn't mean that we have to own it ourselves," I said.

"Suzanne, do you honestly think that you have a prayer of winning this argument with me?" As she asked her question, I saw the line of resolve in her face, and I suddenly knew that there was no point fighting her on it anymore. Besides, did I really want to win this particular argument? It was the perfect beginning to my new life with Jake, and I knew that my mother could easily afford the gesture. She was probably the richest woman in April Springs, and this wouldn't even touch her major holdings. Still, it was the most precious gift she could have given me, besides the love she gave me every day.

"Are you absolutely sure about this?" I asked one last time.

"I'm positive," she said with a twinkle in her eye.

I hugged her, and even though I towered over her, I felt like a little girl again in her arms. "Thank you, Momma. I love you," I whispered.

"I know you do, and I love you at least as much right back," Momma said.

Then I felt Jake's arms enfold us both. "Wow, you surely just won the contest of best wedding present ever," he said with a laugh.

"Good. I always enjoy coming in first place," Momma said as she extracted herself from our embraces. "Now, I really must be going. I don't trust Phillip alone in the house with that pie, and we haven't had our dinner yet."

"If it were me, it would already be a lost cause," Jake said with a smile. "Thanks again, Dot. For everything."

"It was my pleasure," she said as she started for the door.

"Hang on a second," I said as I grabbed my coat. "I'll walk you out."

"That's not necessary, Suzanne," Momma said.

"No, but I want to do it anyway," I replied. Did she look a

little pleased that I'd forced the issue? Once we were both outside and were walking to her car, I said, "That was truly a spectacular gesture, Momma."

She looked up at me and grinned. "Did you honestly expect anything less from me?"

I had to laugh. "From you? Not a chance. I can't thank you enough for this. It means everything to me. Have a good night."

"You, too."

After my mother was gone, I glanced at the land that was now mine—mine and my husband's, I corrected myself—and then I looked at the cottage. It was the only place in the world where I'd ever truly felt at home, and now I owned it. The emotions were so powerful that I wasn't sure how long it would take me to come to grips with them. This, above all else, was my mother's ultimate seal of approval. After all, she hadn't made the gesture, or even hinted at it, when I'd married Max. She knew as well as I did that this time it was different.

This time I'd done it right.

"That was absolutely delicious," Jake said as he pushed his dessert plate away from him. "Your mother is the supreme pie maker in the universe."

"Don't I know it," I said as I started to gather up the dirty dishes. Despite my best intentions, I'd broken down and had a piece myself. There was no way that I was going to be able to sit there and watch Jake enjoying some without joining him. Maybe I'd start walking to work again. That might help me keep my weight down. I knew that wasn't the ultimate solution, though. We'd both walked plenty on our honeymoon, but I'd still managed to gain three pounds while we'd been away. At least I didn't have any chocolate croissants to tempt me in April Springs.

"Do you need any help with the dishes? The reason I ask is that I'd like to make a few phone calls on behalf of your investigation if you don't."

I grinned at him. "Wow, what a tricky way of getting out of a chore."

"Hey, I can go either way. It's your call," he said, answering my smile with one of his own.

"Go on and make your phone calls. I'll take care of these tonight." His look of satisfaction plummeted when I added, "You can do them tomorrow night."

"Fair enough," he said a little ruefully. "I think I'll step out onto the porch, if you don't mind."

"I'll be here when you're through," I said. I didn't even feel bad about assigning the dishes to him tomorrow. I knew that I'd probably do them then as well, but he didn't have to know that.

As I was putting the last plate on the drying rack, Jake walked back in with a frown on his face.

"Is something wrong?" I asked him.

"That didn't go as smoothly as I'd hoped," he said.

"Who exactly did you call?"

"I pulled a few strings that Simpson doesn't know about," Jake answered.

"Was that wise? You don't want to go out of your way to aggravate him."

"Oh, I don't have to make any special effort to do that. It just seems to come naturally."

"What did you find out?" I asked him as I drained the water in the sink.

"It appears that there's been more going on in Granite Meadows than first meets the eye. My former boss recently assigned a team to investigate the police force there for corruption."

"When did all of this happen?"

"About a month ago," he said.

"So then Alex Tyler could have been a subject of the investigation," I answered heavily.

"It's entirely possible," Jake said. "Suzanne, I don't want you and Grace to go there alone after hearing this, at least not to talk to anyone on the police force. This may be a little beyond the scope of your investigation."

"Do you think it might be true? I never really cared for Alex, but I never dreamed that he was dirty."

"He might not have been," Jake said, scolding me, "and until we have solid evidence otherwise, the man is innocent until proven guilty. Understood?"

I didn't care for my husband's tone of voice, but I could certainly understand it. "Sorry. I didn't mean to jump to any conclusions."

My contriteness hit home with him. "Suzanne, I'm the one who's sorry. I shouldn't have snapped at you. It's just that I hate assuming anything bad when it comes to a cop's honor and integrity."

"Hey, you were right and I was wrong."

"Care to repeat that into my microphone?" he asked with a grin as he held a pretend one forward.

"Not a chance. So, what do we do about this new twist? Do we just drop that part of the investigation and let the state police worry about it?"

"I'm not sure yet," Jake said. "I'd really like to sleep on it before I give you an answer."

I stifled a yawn. "That's not a bad idea. Speaking of sleeping, I have to get up pretty early tomorrow morning."

"Bedtime it is, then," Jake said as he stretched for a moment.

I put a hand on his chest. "Hang on there, mister. I know that you keep regular business hours. There's no way that you need to keep my sleep schedule. You can't. It will wear you out in no time. Just because I'm going to sleep doesn't mean that you have to. I have a decent library here, and there's always television if you get tired of reading."

"I never get tired of reading," Jake said. "Nonetheless, at least for tonight, I'm going to sleep when you do. Okay?"

"Okay, as long as you don't make a habit of it," I said with a grin.

"I'm not making any promises," he said, smiling back at

me.

To my surprise, I had no trouble bouncing out of bed the next morning at an hour that most folks considered the middle of the night. Even though I'd partially adapted my sleeping schedule to what many people considered normal over the past ten days, there had always been something in me that had been dying to get back to my old routine. I kissed Jake's cheek, half expecting him to wake up as I got up, but he just muttered something and fell right back asleep in our bed.

And to be honest, I wasn't all that unhappy about it. I liked my morning rituals, all accomplished while most of the world around me slept. There was something about the solitude of it all that gave me peace knowing that while I worked, the folks I'd be feeding soon were home and safely asleep. Driving down the street toward Donut Hearts, I found myself reveling in the darkness. Soon I'd have the lights on inside, coffee brewing in the pot, and donut batter mixing, but for now, for that moment, I had the night all to myself.

Chapter 9

"Hey there," Emma said later that morning when she finally came for her shift. I'd been there for some time prepping things for the day, and while I'd loved my solitude, it felt good being back with her in the donut shop kitchen again.

"How did it feel to sleep in?" I asked her as I put the finishing touches on the last of my cake dough batters. Working in the donut shop was really two distinct jobs, no matter what most folks believed. The cake donuts were all done with batters, varying the ingredients until we had a nice range of the old-fashioned type of donuts ready to sell. After they were fried and iced, it was time to start on the second stage of our day and make the raised donuts so many of my customers loved. I'd been tempted on more than one occasion to skip making one type or the other over the years, but in the end, I couldn't bring myself to do it. Such was the lot of the donutmaker, a mantle I'd gladly taken on.

She laughed happily, a sound I'd missed lately. "Only you could think that getting up at three in the morning qualifies as sleeping in. How are the cake donuts doing? Do you need any help with anything?"

"Emma, I could make most of these recipes in my sleep. When I lost my recipe book to that fire, it felt pretty tragic to me at the time, but mostly it was from the sentimental value. That's not discounting how lucky I felt when I found out that your mother had made a copy for herself surreptitiously."

"Then I'll leave you to it and get started setting up the front," Emma replied as she ducked back out of the kitchen. I continued to drop different rings of batter into the hot oil, flipping them, retrieving them, and then icing them as she set things up for our day out front. When I'd finished the cake donuts, I went out and joined her. "How's it going out here?"

"We're all set," Emma replied as she finished cleaning the

glass on the last of the display cases. "Are the cake donuts finished?"

"They're ready to rack, and you can get started on your first round of dishes."

"I'm raring to go," she said with a smile. "I enjoyed running this place while you were gone, but I can't wait to go back to my own little world. When you're here, all I care about is seeing the bottom of that sink after the last of the dirty racks and pans are all washed."

"Then let's get to it."

As Emma worked on the massive pile of dirty racks, pans, utensils, and mixing bowls I'd created earlier, I started measuring out the flour, water, and yeast to get my raised donuts going. It was always a race to see if I'd finish before or after she did, but today it was no contest, even with the head start I'd had. That girl flew through those dishes in a flash, and she had a full two minutes to wait for me until the dough was ready to go through its first proofing stage.

"Wow, you were really quick today," I said as I washed my hands in the big sink she'd so recently finished with. "I thought you might lose a step or two, given that you had a late start."

"No, ma'am. You know me; I'm always on my game," she replied. "I know it's getting really chilly, but I'd still love to go outside for our break."

"You don't have to convince me. I'm looking forward to the brisk air. Maybe it will help wake me the rest of the way up," I said as I stifled a yawn. "It's always a little tough shifting my hours back after I've been off, and it doesn't seem to be getting any easier as the months and years go by."

"Well, you can't blame old age for it, because I have problems when I do it, too," Emma said as we walked out front together, bundled up in our own warm jackets.

"Who said anything about old age?" I asked her with a grin.

"Nobody. No one said anything about that at all," she said, doing her best to keep a straight face.

It lasted three seconds before we both started laughing.

"I've missed you, Suzanne," Emma said as I unlocked the front door.

"Right back at you, kiddo," I answered.

"Is that snow?" I asked as I held a hand out into the night. "It can't be. It's way too early for that."

"Tell that to the sky," Emma said as she reached out and caught a flake on her tongue.

"I wonder how much we'll get?"

"Hang on a second," Emma said, and then she pulled out her phone and tapped a few buttons. "It's not supposed to accumulate. As a matter of fact, it will likely all be gone by dawn."

"That's pretty amazing," I said.

"Not really," Emma answered. "There's just not that much moisture in the system to get much more than a few flurries."

"I'm not talking about the snow, I mean the fact that you can access that kind of information with your cellphone."

"Yes, this century is truly amazing," Emma said with a grin as she put her phone back into her pocket. "There are all kinds of New Age gizmos folks from your time never had."

"You know what I mean. Or maybe you don't. When I was growing up, the only way your folks had to get in touch with you was to yell out the back door. In the summer, we were often gone from breakfast until it was time for dinner that night, and nobody gave it a second thought. Now if someone doesn't answer a text message within thirty seconds, everyone panics."

"It has its pluses and minuses," Emma said. "Listen, there's something I'd like to talk to you about. I'm really sorry I dragged the donut shop into this murder investigation."

"Emma, don't ever apologize for that. You had every right in the world not to go out with Alex Tyler, and you can't hold yourself responsible for the way he reacted to your rejection."

"That's what my mother keeps telling me, too. Honestly, I

know in my head that you're right, but I can't help wondering how things might have worked out differently if I'd just said yes."

"You'll drive yourself crazy thinking like that," I said. "How could you possibly know that someone would use a cup of our coffee to poison the man after you turned him down for a date?"

"I understand that there's no way I could have known that," she agreed. "Still, it doesn't make it any easier to accept. Have you had any luck so far in your investigation?"

"We've just gotten started," I said. "There are a few factors that are making this case more difficult for us than anything Grace and I have ever tackled before."

"I still can't believe that Grace is helping you," Emma said as the snow continued to fall, though it had eased up considerably since we'd come outside.

"Why shouldn't she? We almost always work together."

"Maybe so, but that was before you got married to a hunky ex-state policeman," Emma reminded me.

"Jake's working for the mayor as an independent investigator on the case," I said. "There are some tasks that he can't do that Grace and I can, though."

"That's hard to believe," Emma said, and then she quickly slapped a hand over her mouth. "I didn't mean that the way it must have sounded."

"No worries, Emma. I fully realize that there are a great many things that Jake can do that Grace and I can't, but there are at least a few jobs that no one else can do as well as we can, either."

"I'm dying to hear an example or two," Emma said.

"Well, for starters, Grace and I usually know the people involved, so that gives us an edge from the start. Then there's the fact that we aren't intimidating, so a lot of people drop their guards around us. It's a lot different talking to a couple of nosy women than it is a police officer, in whatever form he might take."

"I never really thought about it that way before."

Emma chewed on her thumbnail for a moment, and I knew from experience that there was something else on her mind. "Is there something you want to talk to me about?" I asked her.

"No. I'm fine."

"Emma, you know that you can discuss anything with me, and I mean anything."

"Usually you are right, but this is different," she said. "It's about Alex's murder. Dad found out something last night, and he's holding it back from Jake. Suzanne, I'm torn between loyalty to my dad and the way I feel about you. It's not fair what he's doing, but I'm not sure that gives me the right to disclose his secrets."

"Emma, you shouldn't tell me anything that you're not comfortable sharing," I said after a moment's thought.

"Do you think Jake would feel the same way about it as you do?"

"Not a chance," I answered with a smile. "If I'm sure of anything, it's that Jake would urge your father to share anything he uncovered with the police at the soonest possible instant."

"That's what I was afraid of. Do you think Jake will lock my dad up if he finds out he's holding something back?"

"I don't know," I answered.

Emma actually looked a little disappointed at my response. "Emma, do you *want* your father to go to jail?"

"For protecting a source? Are you kidding me? He'd be in heaven if that happened! Jake would be doing him a huge favor if he locked him up for that."

It was an interesting way of looking at things, that was for sure. "I don't even know how to respond to that."

"You don't have to," Emma said as she rubbed her hands together. "Would you have any interest in cutting our break short and making a little hot cocoa?"

I stood and clapped my hands together. I'd neglected to bring my gloves or my heavy coat, so I was chilled pretty thoroughly by then as well. "That sounds like an excellent idea."

As we moved back inside, Emma said, "Thanks, Suzanne."

"For what, cutting our break short? It sounds good to me, too."

"No, I'm talking about not pressing me about what Dad is hiding from everyone."

"That's on his conscience and yours, not mine," I said with a grin.

"I'm not exactly thrilled with you putting it that way," Emma said with a wry smile of her own.

"That's what it all boils down to in the end, though, isn't it?"

"I suppose so," she said.

As we made our special blend of hot chocolate together, I kept having the feeling that Emma was about to divulge the information she was keeping from me, but I didn't press her. I knew that she had to make up her own mind, and nudging her would only make her that much more reluctant to share it with me. If I bided my time, though, there was a decent chance that she'd eventually tell me.

At least that was what I hoped would happen.

But until that time came, there were donuts to make, a shop to open, and folks to serve; it was plenty enough to occupy our thoughts and time until Emma decided to share with me, or not.

Chapter 10

"What on earth are you doing here this early in the morning?" I asked Jake with a grin as I opened the front door to welcome him as my first customer of the day.

"I've been awake a few hours," he admitted. "Man, this place smells wonderful first thing in the morning. I'll have one plain glazed and one plain cake donut, please. Oh, and some coffee would be nice, too. How do I do this? Do I pay you now, or should we set up a tab for me?" he asked as he reached for his wallet.

"Put your money away. You don't have to pay for anything here," I said as I filled his order, grabbing one each of our simplest donuts for him. "I told you before that going to bed that early would throw off your sleep schedule."

"And you were right," Jake said with a smile. "I tried to get into my temporary office at the police station, but Stephen wasn't there yet, and he's the only one with a key."

"You could have just broken in," I said with a smile as I handed him his coffee. "Why don't you sit here by me?"

"Don't mind if I do," Jake said as he took the spot closest to the register. "This is excellent," he added after taking a bite of the glazed donut. "It's still warm."

"I know. That's when I like them best. So, how are we going to handle our schedules from now on?" I asked him as I grabbed a cup of coffee for myself. I was tempted to have a donut with him as well, but that would lead to me having to buy the next size up in jeans quickly enough. I had to save my treats for the new donut recipes I tried. Come to think of it, maybe that was why I was constantly offering my customers new tasty things to sample.

"Don't worry. We'll work it out. Chances are I'll be staying up past eight p.m. from here on out, though. Do you mind?"

"Mind? I'm the one who tried to get you to do it last night, remember?" I leaned over and kissed his cheek. "It was a sweet gesture, though, no matter how impractical it might have been."

"How does it feel to be back behind the counter again?" he asked after taking another sip of his coffee.

"It's where I belong," I said as I looked around the place. "You know, I never imagined that is how my life would turn out, but I'm sure glad that it all worked out that way."

"I'm happy for you," Jake said. He took a hearty bite of the cake donut and then he smiled again. "I don't know how to decide which one is my favorite."

"Do like I do," I said. "My first choice is always the one I'm eating at the time."

"That system will do fine until I can come up with something else. So, what are your plans after you shut down for the day? Are you and Grace heading back to Granite Meadows?"

"I don't see that we have much choice," I replied. "You said you were going to sleep on it to see if you could come up with something. Did you have any luck?"

"I've been pondering the situation for the past hour, and I think you should—"

I didn't get a chance to hear what he thought, though. Stephen Grant, the acting police chief of April Springs, walked into the donut shop with a grin. "I heard you were looking for me. Sorry about that. I was up late last night helping out on a call."

"Was it anything serious?" Jake asked him eagerly. "You know, if you ever need backup, I'm just a phone call away, and now that I'm living here full time, I'd be happy to lend a hand whenever you need it."

Wow, he sounded really eager when he offered his help. Was Jake missing his old job already? I couldn't imagine how he didn't. After all, he'd had an important position where folks depended on him, and working as a freelance investigator couldn't be nearly as satisfying to him. That was going to be a discussion we'd have to have in the near future.

Just not now.

"It didn't turn out to be anything serious at all. We got a prowler call from Mrs. Jacobson," he said. "She saw a pair of beady eyes in the dark and thought someone was trying to break into her home. Turned out that it was a raccoon eating some dog food she'd spilled feeding her pooches by the back porch."

"Well, in her defense, he *was* wearing a mask," I said with a smile. "Can I get you anything, Chief?"

"Interim chief," he corrected me.

"I'm not saying that," I replied. "Until someone else comes along, you're doing the job, so why shouldn't you at least get the title?"

Chief Grant just shrugged, and then he turned back to Jake and handed him something. "Here's your key. Sorry again about that. You're welcome to look through any files I have on the case, but that's about all I can do for you." In a lower voice, Stephen added, "That's rubbish, of course. I'll do whatever I can to help, but I was told that I had to tell you that first thing."

Jake grinned. "Understood. I'm guessing you and Manfred had a little chat yesterday."

Stephen nodded. "I suppose you could call it that, but if I wasn't allowed to reply, could you really call it a conversation? It was really more like a lecture. The man's not all that fond of you, is he?"

"That's putting it mildly," Jake replied. "No worries. I won't go through him, but I don't mind going around him."

"Given your status, you need to be careful," Stephen said. "I got the distinct impression that he's just dying to shut you down."

"There's no doubt about it, but I've been outsmarting the man for years, and I don't think a change in job titles is going to affect that any. Thanks for the key," Jake finished as he tucked it into his front shirt pocket.

"Glad to do it," he said.

"Care for something while you're here?" I asked him again.

"I really shouldn't," Stephen said with a sigh as he looked at rack after rack of my treats.

"Three quarters of my customers could probably say that, but I'm sure glad that they don't."

"Okay, you twisted my arm," the chief said with a grin. "I'll take one lemon-filled donut and a coffee to go, please." He started to get out his wallet when Jake said, "Don't worry about it. This one's on me."

My new husband winked at me, and I winked right back. Then I told him, "That'll be two dollars and forty-nine cents," as I held out my hand.

Jake looked surprised by my request for payment. "I thought I had carte blanche here."

"You do, but only for what you consume yourself," I said with a smile.

"Fair enough," Jake said as he pulled out his wallet. He handed me three singles as he said, "Keep the change."

"Wow, my very first tip of the day," I said as I put what was left in the tip jar by the register.

"Can I walk you over to the station?" Stephen asked Jake. "I can at least run interference for you with Inspector Simpson." The interim chief hadn't offered to pay in Jake's place, which made me happy. I figured that I might as well start training my new husband from the start, and showing by example was much easier than simply laying out the rules for him.

"See you later," Jake said as he gave me a quick peck.

"Bye," I replied, but I wasn't sure that he'd even heard me. He was already engrossed in a new conversation with Stephen Grant about their mutual cases, and I knew that at least for now, I'd lost him. Jake was like a border collie; he liked and needed to work in order to be happy. I just hoped that once this case was finished, he'd find something that fulfilled him in April Springs. I knew some folks believed that a happy wife meant a happy life, but I liked to think of it as a happy man made for a happy plan. It wasn't quite as good a rhyme as the standard, but it worked for me. It suddenly occurred to me that he hadn't shared his idea with me about approaching the situation in Granite Meadows. I'd have to get it from him later, though. Traffic in Donut Hearts was starting to pick up, and it took everything I had to keep up with the demand.

Twenty minutes later, after I'd served several of my regulars, the mayor himself walked in. "George, it's good to see you," I said, and after hesitating a moment, I decided that the situation warranted a hug, though I fully realized that it wasn't anywhere near the mayor's comfort zone.

"You, too. Did you bring me anything back from Paris?" he asked me with a grin.

I was ready for him and for anyone else who happened to ask me that question. "As a matter of fact, I did," I said as I handed him a euro coin. Jake and I had forgotten to exchange them for US dollars when we'd gotten back into the country, so we'd decided to use them as tokens when we got back to town instead. They made interesting presents for folks who had never been out of the States, and besides, they were a great deal less expensive than any souvenirs we could have bought. "Here you go."

The mayor took the coin with interest and studied it for a moment before replying. "It's kind of neat, isn't it? Thanks. That's a thoughtful gift," he said as he pocketed the coin.

I felt a little bad about that, since we'd put no thought into it at all, but he didn't have to know that. "Are you here for a treat? Is Polly gone again?"

"I'm afraid that's over," George said sadly.

"No! What happened? You two were perfect for each other," I said.

"Maybe so, but we both decided that a long-distance relationship wasn't going to work at our age. She's selling her house and moving in with her daughter to help take care of her kids. I can't say that I didn't see it coming, but it doesn't make it any easier to take. Now I'm not only out a lady friend, but I also have to look for a new secretary, too.

Do you have any thoughts?"

"For a replacement secretary or a new girlfriend?" I asked him with a gentle smile.

"Maybe both," he answered in kind. I knew that George was upset, but I was glad to see that he wasn't going to let it affect his disposition.

"Don't look at me," I said. "I'm a happily married woman and the proud owner of a donut shop, so I strike out on both counts."

He shook his head as he laughed. "I wasn't asking you to fill either position. I just figured you might know of someone, being how you have your finger on the pulse of April Springs."

"I'm not sure I'd say that," I answered.

"Suzanne, most folks find their way into this place sooner or later. Think about it."

"Okay, but in the meantime, how are you going to manage at the office? According to what you've told me in the past, Polly pretty much ran the place."

"I'm not quite the figurehead I may have let on," George said. "I think I can keep things together for the time being. Besides, one of the secretaries from the Register of Deeds has volunteered to help out until I can find someone more permanent."

"It wouldn't be Harriet Light by any chance, would it?" I asked him slyly.

"As a matter of fact it was. How did you know that?"

I had to laugh. "George, that woman has had a crush on you for as long as I can remember. Surely you knew that, didn't you?"

"Harriet? Why, I'm at least twenty years older than she is. The thought never even crossed my mind. What would people think?"

"I personally believe that they'd applaud. George, it's not like she's a teenager. Harriet is a widow in her forties. No one's going to bat an eye if you two start going out."

"I'm not at all sure about that," he said. "Let's change the subject, if that's okay with you."

"Hey, you're the one who brought it up. Can I get you something, or did you just come by for some good conversation?"

He studied the display cases for a moment before he ordered, though I could easily guess what he was about to have.

George surprised me, though. "I'll have a glazed donut with chocolate sprinkles and a chocolate milk, but I'd better get it to go. I need to wade through a pile of paperwork now that Polly's quit her job."

"You're kidding me," I said, surprised by his request.

"Why would you be surprised that I'd be overwhelmed with work with my secretary gone?"

"I'm talking about the donut and drink order," I said. "Are you sure that's what you'd like?"

"What can I say? I feel like shaking things up a little."

"Good for you," I said as I filled his order.

After I made change for him, I watched him leave the shop. George didn't act all that upset about Polly's departure, and I had to wonder if there was more to the story than he was letting on. Should I have pried a little more? Had she asked him to move with her? Had he begged her to stay? I might never know, because if George had wanted to tell me more, he would have volunteered the information. It appeared that he was doing his best to move on with his life, so I decided that I was going to respect his wishes.

At least I was going to try to.

Only time would tell if I'd be able to do it or not.

I was still musing about our conversation when Brandon Morgan walked into the donut shop.

I didn't realize it at the time, but things were about to get really interesting.

Chapter 11

"I thought you hated donuts," I said with a smile as Brandon came into my shop.

"No, not really," he said, trying his best to match mine, but failing miserably.

"Really. The reason I say that is because I'm pretty sure that was you I saw picketing out front when I had my problems with Lester Moorefield a few years back," I said. That particular confrontation hadn't ended well for Lester, but not because of anything that I'd done, though some of the townsfolk had suspected that I might have had a hand in the radio show host's demise.

"Suzanne, that was a long time ago. I'm a big enough man to admit when I've made a mistake, and I'm sorry to say that I was wrong to do what I did back then. What do you say? Can we let bygones be bygones? How about a donut?"

"Sure, I'm not one to hold grudges. What would you like?"

He studied the display case. "What's the healthiest donut you have on the menu?"

That was easy. Back before Grace had come around to the joys of my calorie-laden donut treats, I'd made a few special ones just for her. "Let's see. Today I've got vegan vanilla cake and a blueberry banana that uses yogurt."

"Wow. Seriously?"

"You'd be surprised by how many folks like to indulge a little but still maintain a modicum of healthy ingredients."

"How do they taste?" he asked as he looked at them skeptically.

"Tell you what. I'll let you taste a bite of each first. If you don't like either one of them, you don't have to pay me a cent."

"But if I do?"

"Then you pay double what they cost anyone else," I said with a grin.

"Why don't I just buy them outright from you instead?"

Brandon asked.

"You could certainly do that if you'd like to, but I'm trying to prove a point here. Just because something's healthy doesn't mean that it can't taste good, too."

"If you feel that way, then why do you serve so many selections of the unhealthy options?"

Was he seriously going to stand there in my donut shop and argue with me about my offerings? "Brandon, I never recommended a steady diet of my fare to anyone, but every now and then it feels good to indulge. So, what do you say? Are you willing to take me up on my offer? How lucky are you feeling?"

"What's to keep me from lying?" he asked.

"Not a thing in the world but your conscience," I said.

"Why not? What have I got to lose?" he asked.

"Five bucks, from where I'm standing," I said with a smile as I retrieved one of each of the donuts we'd just been discussing.

He didn't want to like them. I could see it in his gaze as he studied my offerings.

I watched as a sense of amazement covered his face when he took his first bite. "Say, this is really tasty."

"I told you so. Now try the other one."

Brandon took a bite of that one as well, and then he frowned as he shook his head.

"What's the matter, don't you like it?" I asked. I'd been sure that I'd offered him two winners.

"I don't like it, I love it."

"Then why the frown?"

"I owe you five bucks," Brandon said as he dug out his wallet and slid a five across the counter. "You know what? I don't even mind being proven wrong."

"Good for you," I said. "How about if I throw in one more of each donut to go? That way you're getting your money's worth, and I still get to make my point."

"No, a bet's a bet. You won fair and square," he said. "How about some coffee?"

"Do you actually drink that? Isn't it bad for you, too?"

"Not in moderation," he said. "Speaking of coffee, that was too bad about how Alex Tyler died. Who would have dreamed that he drank poisoned coffee from your donut shop."

"I'm sure that it wasn't poisoned when it left here," I said, immediately going on the defensive.

"No doubt you're right," he said. "Does your boyfriend have any idea who might have done it?"

"Haven't you heard?" I asked him as I showed him my wedding ring. "He's my husband now."

"Congratulations," Brandon said automatically. "He's still working on the case, though, isn't he?"

"In a manner of speaking," I said.

"Does he have any leads yet?" Brandon asked me, his voice lowered to a near whisper, as though he were having trouble getting the words out.

It was rather curious behavior, and I had to call him on it. "Why all of the sudden interest in what happened to the new police chief?"

"What do you mean?" Brandon definitely looked a little guilty when I'd asked. "We're just talking."

"Maybe so, but the last time you were within a hundred yards of Donut Hearts, you were holding a sign that said, 'Donuts Kill!' Now you're in here eating my treats and asking me questions about a murder that doesn't concern you. Or does it?"

"Like I said, I'm just making polite conversation," he said. "Can I get these to go? I need to be somewhere."

"Sure thing," I said.

As I started to bag his partially eaten donuts, Emma came in through the kitchen. "Suzanne, we're running low on flour. Would you like me to call—?" The second she saw Brandon, she faltered, and her sentence died in the air mid-delivery.

"I already called him," I said. "More is on the way."

"Good. Fine. I'll just get back to work, then." My

assistant was gone in an instant, and Brandon was looking in her direction with a curious expression that defied explanation.

"Thanks for the donuts," he said as he held up the bag and shook it a little.

"Come back anytime," I said.

The moment he was gone, I opened the door to the kitchen. "Emma, would you mind coming here for a second?" If I stood in the doorway, I could carry on a conversation with her and still watch the front.

"What's up, boss?"

"That's what I want to know. The instant you saw that Brandon Morgan was in the donut shop, you couldn't get out of the front fast enough. Do you two have some kind of history that I don't know about?"

"Me and Brandon? Yuck. You're kidding, right?"

"Well, there's got to be some reason you acted so weird around him." I thought about it for another moment, and then I made an educated guess. "He's on your dad's list of suspects, isn't he?"

Her expression told me that I'd scored a direct hit. "What? No. I never said that. No way."

"Emma," I said softly. "I won't tell anyone where I got my information."

"I can't," she said. The way her voice quivered, I could tell that she was on the edge of tears.

"That's okay. You don't have to tell me a thing."

"Dad would kill me," she said, a pleading quality in her voice that it pained me to hear.

"I get it. We're good." I closed the door and faced the counter. While Emma hadn't confirmed anything outright, I was pretty sure that I was on the money.

At that point, I did what any self-respecting concerned citizen would do.

I decided to call the police.

Well, not just any police. I knew that my husband had recently retired from being an officer of the law, but he was still working as a cop, and I wasn't certain that I could ever think of him any other way. "Jake, I've got a hot tip for you."

"I'll take it," he said. "I'm still trying to get settled in over here. Evidently Manfred is on the move, because he hasn't been in here all morning. What have you got?"

"You should look for some kind of connection between Alex Tyler and Brandon Morgan."

There was dead silence on the other end of the line for a few moments, and then Jake finally spoke. "How did you know about that?"

"About what?"

"While we were in Paris," Jake explained, "Alex arrested Brandon for speeding, and the two of them got into a pretty ugly confrontation right on the street. I've got him on my list of folks to interview. How did you know about him? Don't tell me. Emma told you, didn't she?"

I knew that I was dancing close to the edge of the truth by not telling him everything, but I had to protect Emma's involvement, too. I decided to slant my response to deflect Jake's suspicion of my assistant. "As a matter of fact, the man just paraded into the donut shop asking questions about Alex's murder, and he wanted an update on the progress you were making on the case."

"What's so odd about someone coming into Donut Hearts? I thought that most of the town ate there sooner or later. As for the case, the whole town's talking about it, so that doesn't make Brandon Morgan all that different if he wants to hear about how we're doing."

"The thing is, though, Brandon was one of the protesters outside the shop when I was battling Lester Moorefield," I explained. "Seeing him in here is like finding a lump of coal in a bag of marshmallows. He just didn't belong."

"Okay, I get it. Maybe I'll ask him about it when I speak with him later today. Thanks for the tip."

"In the spirit of sharing, is there anyone else in April Springs you're looking at particularly closely?"

Jake paused another moment before answering. "I thought you were focusing on Granite Meadows and I was handling April Springs?"

"That's the plan, but surely there's going to be some overlap. What am I supposed to do when one of your suspects walks in and starts asking questions like Brandon just did?"

"That's a fair point. I can't tell you anything directly. You know that, don't you?"

"Well, can you at least give me a hint?"

"How about this? If anyone comes in asking questions about Alex, let me know about it, pronto."

"You seriously aren't going to at least give me any idea about who I need to be careful around?"

"Suzanne, we're both working on a murder investigation. You should be careful about everyone you see until we catch the killer."

"I know that," I said. I saw a family of four approaching the shop. "I've got to go."

"Don't be cross with me," he said plaintively.

"I'm not. I'm just trying to run a business." I hung up on him before I could say something that I would probably regret. I knew that he was just doing his job and that sometimes it precluded him from telling me everything he knew, even though I didn't have that kind of caveat.

That didn't mean that I had to like it.

Apparently there were going to be more things for us to get used to in our married life than most couples had to go through.

I knew that I'd be fine once I had a little time to cool down.

In the meantime, I had customers to serve.

Chapter 12

"Hey there," Jake said, walking in just as I was about to close Donut Hearts for the day. I'd sent Emma home early in reward for covering for me while I'd been on my honeymoon, and she'd gladly accepted the goodwill gesture. I'd been there alone for the past half hour, and of course, we'd gotten busy just moments after Emma had gone on her way. "Are you still open?"

"I was just about to lock up," I said, and then I did exactly that, flipping the sign to let my customers know that there were no more donuts, at least for that day. "I'm now officially closed, but I have a few things I have to take care of before I can leave."

"Can I give you a hand with anything?" It was a nice gesture, and I decided to take him up on his generous offer.

"How do you feel about sweeping?" I asked him with a smile. I'd gotten over my little snit. After all, he was just doing his job. I had no right resenting the fact that he couldn't share everything he learned on a case with me.

"As a matter of fact, my mother made sure I knew how to operate a broom firsthand since I was tall enough to hold one in my hands."

"Excellent," I said as I handed him our broom. I'd already cleaned the tables in anticipation of closing up shop, so it was quick work to flip the chairs over and get them off the floor. "If you could sweep up, I can get started on running reports for the day's totals."

"After I finish this," he said as he began to sweep, "I'd be happy to do the dishes as well."

"Be careful about how generous your offer is. You might go on the payroll when you're not looking," I said happily. "Besides, don't you already have a job? You're investigating Alex Tyler's murder, remember?"

"I'm not likely to forget it, but that doesn't mean that I'm not allowed to take a lunch break," Jake said as he collected the remnants of dropped donuts, forgotten napkins, and other detritus that found its way to the floor in the course of a typical day.

"And you really want to spend it helping me clean up my shop?"

"As long as you're here, that's where I want to be."

"I feel the exact same way about you."

"Well, I should hope so," he said with a grin as he finished sweeping up the discards and putting everything in the closest trash can. "Now, how about those dishes?"

"As much as I appreciate your offer, I just have a few trays left to do in back, and I can knock them out in no time while the report is running." I studied the display cases and realized that I had more than three dozen donuts left. "Either I made too many donuts this morning, or my customer base is dropping way off."

"How can you possibly know that without checking your numbers?"

"Oh, I'll go ahead and run the report on the register, but I don't need it to tell me that things have slacked off around here," I said as I turned the key in the register lock to its report setting. After I hit a few other buttons, it started spitting out the day's take, dividing it into neat little segments. Checking the cash we had on hand, I jotted the number down just as the report finished running. I knew that there were newer, much more modern cash registers that did everything electronically, but I liked this system better. I could rely on the numbers printed on the tape more than I could on ones flashing past on a display. "Well, that's settled."

"What is?"

"According to this, my sales are down over fifteen percent since we got married."

"You honestly can't think that there's a cause and effect to your slump, can you?" he asked, clearly concerned about my response.

"No, I have a hunch that it has more to do with the new

chief of police being poisoned with Donut Hearts coffee than it does with our nuptials," I said.

"It wasn't the coffee that killed him," Jake said as he put the broom away.

"Excuse me?"

"I said that it wasn't the coffee that was poisoned," Jake replied.

"Seriously? That's wonderful news," I said gleefully. "How soon can we tell folks that Donut Hearts is in the clear?"

"It's not quite that simple, I'm afraid," he said.

"What's the catch? If it wasn't my coffee or my donuts that killed Alex, then no one from my shop should be a suspect in anyone's mind."

"While it's true that your coffee wasn't poisoned, that doesn't mean that the cup itself was free from suspicion," he explained.

"You've got to be kidding me," I said, feeling the air go out of my sails.

"I wish I were, but I don't joke around about things like that. According to the lab, someone coated the interior of the cup with a common household cleaning product that is fairly toxic. When the coffee was added, the poison dissolved, killing Alex after he ingested it."

"How can they possibly know that?"

"They tested the sides of the cup that didn't come into contact with any liquid," Jake said. "The traces were still there."

"Then what difference does it make?" I asked, feeling truly dejected now. "Something bought here was still used to commit murder, whether it was the liquid itself or the vessel that was used to transport it. Either way, I'm in the same fix that I was in before."

"Suzanne, this new information implies a few things about the killer, don't you think? The evidence might not clear any of the Donut Hearts staff, but it can't help but assist us with the case."

"If you say so," I said as I made out the bank deposit slip. "Either way, my receipts are still down."

"I wish there was something I could do about that, but we both know that there's not."

"You could find the killer and take the heat off me," I said as I started boxing up leftover donuts. I couldn't take them to the church where I usually dropped them off to feed the less fortunate of April Springs. Emma had told me that we'd worn out our welcome delivering too many in the recent past. That left throwing them away, something I truly hated to do, or using them as bribes during the course of my further investigation. At least I'd have some available for that today, though I wasn't exactly sure who I could use them on.

"I'm doing my best," he said, clearly upset by the tone this conversation had suddenly taken. "Listen, I'm really sorry about earlier."

The poor man was trying to solve this murder under the most exasperating circumstances, and here I was, selfishly piling on. That was about to change. He deserved my support, not my disapproval. "I'm not exactly being fair to you, am I?" I asked as I kissed him on the cheek. "You are right to withhold whatever you decide from me while you're working on official police business."

"Wow, I never thought I'd get off the hook that easily," Jake said with a smile.

"Don't celebrate too much just yet. That still doesn't mean that you should keep anything from me that's not directly related to Alex Tyler's murder investigation. I've already been through one marriage full of lies, secrets, and hidden agendas, and I'm not about to go through another one."

"Completely understood," Jake said, and to my surprise, he swept me up in his arms. "But you should know that I'm not Max. I've never been like him, and I never will be. You can take that to the bank."

"I realize that," I said, grinning. "Now let me go. I have work to do."

"Your wish is my command," he said as he released me.

"What did I just say about lying to me?" I asked him happily.

"Suzanne, you have to at least allow me to embellish every now and then. Otherwise what fun would it be?"

"I suppose you're right," I said. "Seriously, though, I know that you didn't come here to help me clean up the donut shop. What's your real reason for just showing up?"

"Isn't the new information about the coffee cup being tainted enough of a justification for me to come by?" Jake asked me.

"We both know that you could have done that with one phone call."

Jake frowned for a moment before he spoke again. "How about the fact that I missed my bride? Is that cause enough?"

"Of course it is, but why do I keep thinking that there's another shoe waiting to drop?"

To my surprise, my husband laughed happily, a sound that filled me with great joy. Max and I hadn't laughed nearly enough during our time together. The drama had outweighed the happiness by far, but Jake and I weren't about to make that same particular mistake. Jake had been quite a bit more somber when I'd first known him, but leaving his position as a state police inspector had changed him, lightening his load—and his mood—considerably. There was more room for smiles, for laughter, for sheer joy now, and I knew from those things, more than anything else, that him quitting had been the absolute right thing to do. "You know me too well. Okay, I'll lay all of my cards out on the table. I don't want you and Grace going back to Granite Meadows and talking to those cops."

"But Jake, we have to; you can't do it yourself. You've been limited to working in April Springs," I protested.

"You know what? I don't care anymore. Simpson might not like it, but I'm not really sure what he can do about it, and that's just going to come into play if he manages to catch me doing it."

"Do you know something? You're starting to sound more

and more like me every day," I said.

"Isn't that a good thing?"

"You know it is. I just don't want you to burn any bridges on my account."

"Suzanne, if they are burning, it's because I intentionally set them on fire. I'm going to Granite Meadows with you, whether you like it or not."

"I like it just fine," I said. "I'm not sure what Grace is going to think, though."

"Does she really have a problem with me tagging along on your investigations?" Jake asked me.

"We both know that if you're there, you'll be doing more than tagging along. No offense, but you tend to jump in and take over during these things, Jake."

"What can I say? Old habits die hard, but I think that's exactly what is needed in this case. You both need to realize that none of these cops are going to talk to you if I'm not there with you."

"Hang on a second. They won't be under any obligation to speak with you, either, even if you do have official status in the case in April Springs. Your jurisdiction ends at the town's limits now."

"Maybe so, but at least we speak the same language. Now, we can spend more time arguing about it, or you can unlock the front door and let Grace inside."

I looked out front and sure enough, there was my partner in crime, waiting to be let in. "Let's see what she has to say before we make any decisions," I suggested as I let her in.

Once I explained the new game plan to Grace, she looked a little surprised. "Suzanne, of course we need Jake with us. How else are we going to get anyone in law enforcement to say boo to us otherwise?"

"Then that's settled," Jake said. "I'm coming with you."

"I guess you are," I said. "Now make yourself useful and grab those donuts."

"What do we need these for?" Jake asked me as he dutifully picked up all three boxes.

"We're going to use them for bribes," I said happily. "You don't have any problem with that, do you?"

"No, ma'am. Not one little bit. There are bad bribes, and then there are good ones." He took a deep whiff of my donuts and smiled. "These are good ones."

"Excellent," I said. "Then after we stop off at the bank so I can make my deposit, the three of us are heading to Granite Meadows to investigate."

"The more, the merrier, I say," Grace said happily.

It appeared that the three of us were beginning to form a new team, two amateur sleuths and one ex-cop. It was reminiscent of when George had worked with us before becoming mayor, but I liked this scenario better.

After all, I was with my husband and my best friend.

Chapter 13

"At least the snow finally stopped," I said as I looked out the front windshield of the Jeep at the wet road in front of us.

"What are you talking about? When was it snowing?" Grace asked me from the passenger seat. Jake was once again in back, and I noticed that he'd found a way to sit with his legs positioned that didn't confine him nearly as much as I'd been afraid it would.

"No doubt you were still asleep," I said. "It doesn't matter, since it didn't amount to much."

"I saw some flurries early on," Jake added. "It looked really pretty coming down in the night sky with just the lights from the park illuminating it. I had a warm fire going inside, too, so it was pretty cozy."

"What time did you get up?" Grace asked as she looked around at him.

"The real question is what time did he get to bed," I said.

"You aren't seriously trying to keep your wife's hours, are you?" Grace asked him. "Jake, it will kill you if you try to do that."

"I don't plan on making a regular habit of it," Jake said in his defense. "I just thought it would be nice to do it the first night we were back in town."

"That's sweet," Grace said with a smile.

"I'd like to think so," he answered.

"So, what's our order of attack?" I asked as we made our way to Granite Meadows.

"Do you really think of this as a battle plan?" Jake asked. "You bet I do."

"Me, too," Grace added.

"Hey, I'm not criticizing; I'm impressed," he said. Jake was smart enough not to comment on it any further. "I don't see any way around it. We have to go to the police station first, don't we?"

"I think so, since that's the real motivation behind you

going with us in the first place," I replied.

"I wouldn't say that it's the *only* reason," Jake said.

"It's right up there, though, isn't it?" Grace asked. "Otherwise, your new bride and I are perfectly capable of running our own investigation without you."

"No one ever said otherwise," Jake answered solemnly, which seemed to placate Grace. She was clearly a little bit defensive about what we did.

"And they'd better not start," she said.

It was time to defuse the situation. "The real question is how do we approach Officer Durant?"

"We could always bribe him with donuts. I've heard that cops have an affinity for that sort of thing," Grace said, smiling a little too brightly at Jake.

"It's true sometimes, but it's mostly on a case-by-case basis," Jake conceded. "Still, it might not be a bad way to approach him if Plan A doesn't work."

"Do we actually have a Plan A?" I asked him as I glanced at him in the rearview mirror. Then I turned to Grace as I said, "Wow, we've never had a Plan A before. That kind of implies that there's a Plan B, C, and so forth, doesn't it?" I knew that I wasn't helping the situation, but I couldn't seem to stop myself.

At least Jake had the decency to laugh right along with us. "Plan A, at least in my mind, is that I approach Officer Durant as a fellow law enforcement officer seeking information on an active homicide investigation."

"Where does that leave us, though?" Grace asked.

"Ideally, you'll both be waiting for me in the Jeep," Jake said. Before Grace or I could protest, he added hastily, "This could be really dicey. There are things that a cop might tell another cop that he would never share with a civilian. I'm not trying to exclude either one of you, but the bottom line is that we want information from this guy, and like it or not, he's more likely to give it to me than he is to the two of you."

Grace and I were both silent for a few moments, taking in what Jake had just told us. I knew that he was probably right, and chances were good that Grace knew it as well, but that didn't mean that either one of us had to like it. After all, we weren't making this drive just to keep Jake company. We'd invited him along on our investigation, not the other way around. On the other hand, had we really been the ones issuing the invitation? Jake had basically invited himself, now that I thought about it.

I was about to point that out when Grace spoke up. "How about if we manage to be close by when you talk to him, out of his sightline but within hearing distance? If we can listen to his responses, it might help trigger something for us. Would you try to do at least that much?"

"I'm not sure that I'll be able to get him out of the station," Jake said warily.

"But you'll try, right?" Grace asked again.

"I'll try," he said, the resignation clear in his voice. "But I handle all of the questions, not the two of you."

"Of course," Grace said with a grin that I wasn't completely certain Jake could see. I knew her well enough to realize that if we were within earshot, we'd be within commenting distance as well. I decided to keep that fact to myself, though.

"Okay," Jake said. "If I can't get him to open up with me, you two can try to see what you can get with free donuts. That will be Plan B."

"What's Plan C?" I asked.

"Truthfully, I haven't thought that far ahead yet," Jake admitted. "That's not a problem, is it?"

"Are you kidding?" Grace asked. "We'll be happy to wing it if we need to. Suzanne and I are experts at making things up as we go along. Why should it be any different just because you're here?"

"Remember, we need to tread carefully," Jake said. "There could be a great many reasons Durant doesn't want to talk to us, free donuts or not."

"Like what?" I asked, curious about how the cop's mind worked.

"Let's see. He could feel as though he's protecting his late partner's privacy by refusing to speak with us, for one thing," Jake said. "Then again, if he suspects one of his fellow officers may have had something to do with Alex's demise, he might not be in the mood to share that, either. There could be a dozen reasons for his silence that don't have anything to do directly with his own possible involvement, but I'm hoping that if I push the right buttons, he'll feel obligated to speak with me."

"With us, you mean," Grace prodded him.

"Indirectly, of course, but yes, us," Jake amended.

At least his clarification seemed to mollify Grace a little, so that was something, anyway.

Twenty minutes later, we were in Granite Meadows. The police station was not far from the small downtown area, just as it was in our own April Springs.

After I parked in one of the visitors' spots, Jake said, "I know that this isn't how you two usually operate, but I'd really appreciate it if you'd let me handle this my way."

"That's fine, but we're still coming inside with you, aren't we?" I asked.

"Of course we are," Grace said as she got out without waiting for confirmation.

After looking at Jake's expression, I wasn't so sure that had been his plan, but there was no way that Grace and I were going to stay out in the Jeep while he went inside.

Once we were all out and walking up the sidewalk together, I grabbed Jake's hand and squeezed it. "Don't worry. We won't get in the way."

"Hey, wait for me. I'm carrying a box of donuts," Grace said from behind us.

"Come on, a dozen aren't that heavy," I told her.

"You made them. You should be the one toting them."

"I'd be delighted," I said as I took the box from her with a smile.

"Suzanne, I was just teasing. I didn't mind carrying them."

"No, but you're right. Since I made them, I should be the one who delivers them."

"Only as Plan B, though, remember?" Jake asked us.

"Oh, we remember," Grace said with that impish grin of hers.

I wasn't sure what was about to happen inside, but I was pretty certain that it wasn't going to play out as it must have in Jake's mind when he'd first come up with his original plan.

"I'm here looking for Officer Durant," Jake said as he approached the front duty desk. As promised, Grace and I were holding back to let him have some space, but we still weren't managing to go unnoticed by the folks around us. Much of that was probably directly due to the dozen donuts I was carrying, but a girl can enjoy the attention anyway, can't she? Behind the front area were two rows of desks, mostly unoccupied, though I did spot one officer with her nose buried in paperwork off to one side.

"Sorry, Durant's out on patrol." The man at the desk had barely glanced at Jake before he'd responded. Evidently the magazine he was browsing through was far more riveting than we were.

My husband was clearly not used to being dismissed so casually. "Who's the CO on duty?" Jake asked curtly. "Let me speak with him."

That generated some attention. "The chief is in his office," he said as he looked up at Jake. "And who exactly are you?"

"My name is Jake Bishop, and I'm with the April Springs police. Until recently, I was a special investigator with the state police."

"How bad did you mess up to get busted that far down the food chain?" the man asked, clearly not impressed with Jake's former credentials.

"Just tell the chief he has company," Jake said dismissively, and then he turned his back on the desk officer and started toward us.

"I'm so sorry, Jake," I said softly when he rejoined us. "That had to be hard to take."

"It's nothing I wasn't already expecting," Jake said lightly. "Don't worry about it."

"That's the spirit," Grace said. "Never let them see you cry."

He looked at her oddly for a moment before he answered. "Like I said, it's all good."

Three minutes later, a tall, slender man in uniform came out of one of the nearby offices and approached us. "Are you Jake Bishop?"

"I am," Jake said as he offered his hand.

"Robert Willson," the man said. "I understand you're filling in for Phillip Martin over in April Springs."

"Not really. One of his officers is serving as interim chief. I just agreed to step in and help with the murder investigation. Sorry for your loss."

"I appreciate that," Chief Willson said. "Alex Tyler was a fine officer and a good man."

That hadn't been my impression of him, but then again, I hadn't really known him all that well.

"What can I do for you?" the chief asked.

"I'd like your permission to speak with his former partner, Officer Craig Durant, if I may."

"Sorry, but he's out on patrol," Willson said. "I'm not sure what he could tell you, though. I knew Tyler better than just about anybody around here. I'd be happy to assist you in any way that I can."

"Maybe you could help me, then," Jake said without a glance back in our direction. I had the feeling that the chief didn't even know that we were together.

"I'll do what I can. Come on back to my office and we can talk. We'll have a little more privacy there." So, he must have noticed Grace and me eavesdropping on their conversation after all. Perhaps Chief Willson was a little better than I'd given him credit for so far.

"Out here is fine with me," Jake said gamely.

"Naw, come on back. It won't take a second," the chief insisted.

"Fine," Jake said as he started following the chief back to his office.

If I didn't do something quickly, Grace and I were going to be out of the loop.

"Jake, aren't you forgetting something?" I asked loudly.

He didn't turn around immediately, but the chief did. When we made eye contact, I held up the donuts. "These are for you, Chief."

"What are they, cookies?" he asked as he looked at the box.

"Even better. They are donuts," I replied.

The chief frowned a little. "Isn't that a little too on the nose, bringing a box of donuts to a squad full of cops?"

"Hey, don't blame me. I make them for a living," I said lightly. "If I ran a flower shop, I would have brought you roses. There's no hidden message here. We're all sorry for your loss, and this is the best way we have to show it. We didn't know Alex that well, but he'd already made an impression on the folks in April Springs." It wasn't completely a lie. He'd certainly made an impression on me, just not a good one.

"Sorry. I guess I'm a little touchy about the subject," Chief Willson said as he took the box from me and lifted the lid for a peek. "These look great. Tell you what. I'll put them in the break room. Thanks for your thoughtfulness. Jake, are you ready?"

"Actually, they're with me," Jake said, though I could see that he was pained to admit it.

Chief Willson frowned at him for a moment, glanced quickly at us, and then he looked back at Jake. "Surely they aren't helping you with your investigation, are they?" It was clear that he didn't approve of that prospect at all. Clearly Jake had been right. Without him, we never would have even gotten this far.

"Allow me to introduce them. This is Suzanne," he stumbled a moment before adding, "Hart, my wife, and her best friend, Grace Gauge." We hadn't really discussed the possibility of me taking his last name, and this obviously wasn't the time or place to do it, either. I'd kept Hart through my marriage to Max, and now that I owned a shop called Donut Hearts, it seemed to make more sense to keep it rather than change it to Bishop. Still, that was something we were going to have to discuss somewhere down the line.

"Ladies, it's a pleasure to meet you," he said as he extended a hand to each of us in turn. "Now, if you wouldn't mind waiting over there, we won't be long." It was as blunt a dismissal as I'd received in quite sometime.

I was about to push a little and ask if we might not join them when Grace surprised me by saying, "Take all the time you need. Suzanne and I need to catch up on a few things while you two are talking." She'd said it with that sweet Southern belle accent she used sometimes to get what she wanted. It usually worked.

"We'll be back in a flash," the chief answered, and then he smiled broadly at her.

Grace returned it in kind, and a moment later we were sitting by ourselves.

"Well, that was a little unexpected," I told her softly.

"Suzanne, let's face it. There's no way the police chief was going to speak freely in front of us. At least this way Jake has a chance to come up with something we can use."

"I'd come to that same conclusion myself, but I never expected you to come around so quickly on your own."

"What can I say? I'm reasonable if I'm anything," she said.

I choked back my laughter. "Seriously? You do remember who you're talking to, right?"

"I'm willing to admit that I have my moments," Grace said, "but I can behave myself when the situation calls for it."

"It just doesn't call for it very often, does it?" I asked her with a smile.

"Not so far," she replied with that grin of hers that always made me think that she was up to something, even on those rare occasions when she wasn't. "Besides, I've got an idea about something we can do while we're waiting."

"This ought to be good. I can't wait to hear it," I said.

Chapter 14

"First of all, it entails finding the restroom," Grace said as she stood and approached the cop at the front desk. "Is there a ladies' room nearby?" she asked.

"Not on this floor. You have to go upstairs," he answered abruptly.

"Surely you all don't use that one," Grace said.

"Ours is only for staff and visitors who are here on official business."

"You saw that we came in with Inspector Bishop, didn't you? The chief himself said hello to us. That must count for something."

At that moment, his desk phone rang, but Grace wasn't about to stand quietly by and let him take the call in peace. She raised her eyebrows as she put a hand on his phone before he could answer it, and he finally waved her through. I doubted that her argument had been all that persuasive. He most likely had just wanted to get rid of her. I stood and quickly followed her before the desk cop could protest. He wasn't pleased about me following her, but he didn't try to stop me, so I was okay with his disapproving frown.

"Now what?" I asked Grace softly. "Do you really need to go to the bathroom?"

"We might end up there eventually, but for now, I'd like to speak with *her*." She pointed to the policewoman I'd seen earlier, and we veered off in her direction.

"Excuse me," Grace said to her. "May we ask you something?"

Before she could get anything else out, the woman pointed down the hallway. "Restrooms are on the right down that way. You can't miss them."

"Thanks, but we were wondering if you could tell us anything about Alex Tyler," Grace asked.

The woman, who had FARLEY engraved on her name tag, looked sharply at us both. "Who wants to know?"

"I'm Grace and this is Suzanne," she said warmly. "We met Officer Tyler when he first came to April Springs."

"Did he hit on you, too?" she asked harshly.

"Not me," I said, and Grace acknowledged the same.

Officer Farley shrugged. "What do you know. He told me he was going to turn over a new leaf when he left, but I didn't believe him. Maybe I was wrong about him, after all."

"To be fair, he didn't have that much of an opportunity," I said with the hint of a grin.

"Trust me. He wouldn't have let a chance pass by. I don't know. He said that he was going to make himself into a new man from top to bottom. I just didn't believe him."

"He did try to get my assistant to go out with him, and when she refused, he was pretty persistent pursuing her," I said.

"That sounds more like the Alex I worked with," she said smugly.

"Did you know him very well?" I asked her.

"Are you asking me if we ever dated? No way. Not a chance. I wouldn't date *any* of the men on this force." She didn't even lower her voice as she said it, though perhaps that was because no one else was around.

"Slim pickings around here?" Grace asked sympathetically.

"You don't know the half of it. I have to be able to trust a man before I'll go out with him."

"That's why you don't ever go out, Farley," the desk cop said with a mean laugh. Evidently he was off the phone, and now he was eavesdropping on our conversation. At least he hadn't made a move to throw us out. Not yet, at any rate.

"Nash, nobody's ever going to go out with you, either," she said wearily.

"I happen to have a date tonight," the man said smugly.

"Your mom doesn't count."

"It's not my mom."

"Your sister, either, then," Farley said.

The desk cop waved a hand in dismissal and then turned his attention back to the magazine he'd been reading when we'd first walked in.

"Officer Farley, do you know anybody who might have wanted to hurt Alex?" I asked her.

"Look around. Half the guys on the force had a beef with him," she said.

"Really? What about?" I asked.

She was about to answer when I heard Chief Willson just behind us. "Farley, don't you have a beat to patrol?"

"On my way, sir," she said as she stood and left hurriedly.

Jake joined us all a moment later. What had delayed him?

"Don't mind Officer Farley," Chief Willson said warmly as he turned to us. "She sees conspiracies behind every tree. Did she share any with you this afternoon?"

Grace was about to say something; I could see it in her body language. I decided to beat her to it. "Actually, we were just getting directions to the ladies' room," I said.

"Nothing more than that?" the chief asked me, letting his true interest show for a moment.

"Nothing more," I said with my sweetest smile. Grace wasn't the only one who could use charm to her advantage. I didn't have to always rely on donuts to win people over, though I was the first to admit that they often helped my cause.

"Very good," he said, seemingly satisfied with my response. "What were you doing back here, anyway?"

"We were looking for the ladies' room," I answered.

"I'm afraid you'll have to use the facilities upstairs. No exceptions. I'm sure you understand."

"Completely," I said as I touched Grace's arm lightly. "Come on. Let's go."

Once we were outside, I turned to Jake. "What did you find out?"

"Maybe I should ask you first," he replied. "It appeared that you and Grace were having more success than I was."

"We might have gotten a few things out of Officer Farley before you and the chief showed up," I admitted, "strictly due to Grace's spur-of-the-moment idea."

"What can I say? I came up with Plan C," she said.

"This I've got to hear," Jake said with a smile as we walked back to the Jeep.

I felt as though someone was watching us as we made our way back, and when I turned suddenly to look back at the building, there was movement in the curtains, as though someone had been peeking out from behind them. Could it have been Officer Farley, afraid that she'd told us too much? Or perhaps the police chief wasn't quite as innocent as he'd presented himself to be in all of this. Then again, it could have been nothing more than the heat kicking on and blowing air from the registers into the drapes.

But thinking like that wouldn't do me any good, so I decided to stick with my theory that we'd rattled a few cages on our visit to the police station, and we hadn't even spoken with Officer Durant yet.

"Why don't we wait until we're out of earshot of the police station?" I suggested, and Jake and Grace quickly agreed.

Chapter 15

"You go first," I prodded Jake as we got into the Jeep and left the police station. I wanted to get out of there as fast as we could.

"According to Chief Willson, Alex Tyler was a man without fault and an officer above reproach," Jake started. "I couldn't see his files, because according to his boss, there was nothing to see, but it sounded as though it would have been full of commendations and no signs of the slightest negative."

"You didn't believe that, did you?" I asked him.

"No, I've been a cop long enough to know when someone is trying to hide something from me. I just don't know what it is yet, but I will. What did you two discover?"

"Well, Officer Farley was a little more candid with us than Chief Willson was with you," I said. "Should you tell it, or should I?" I asked Grace.

"Go ahead. I'm sure that you'll do a fine job," Grace said.

"I don't care who tells me, as long as someone does." Jake hesitated, and then he interrupted himself as he looked at me. "Suzanne, why do you keep glancing back here? Do I have something in my teeth?"

"I'm just checking to see if anyone is following us," I admitted.

"Why would they do that?" Grace asked me.

"I could have sworn that someone was watching us as we left the station," I admitted. "Don't mind me. I'm probably just being paranoid."

"Don't sell yourself short. Sometimes being paranoid can keep you alive during a murder investigation," Jake said as he glanced backward as well.

"Nobody's back there," I said, feeling a little silly for bringing it up in the first place.

"Not at the moment, but that's constantly subject to change, so keep checking periodically," Jake said. "Go on. Tell me about Officer Farley."

"She kept stressing that Alex told her he was going to be a changed man when he got to April Springs. At first I thought it might be in his love life, but then she told me that half the cops on the force had a problem with him."

"Did she happen to say why?"

"I was about to ask her that when you and the chief showed up," I said.

"Sorry about that. I just didn't see any reason to keep asking him questions when I knew that he was just going to lie to me."

"Why were you late? The police chief was with us a full minute before you showed up," I asked him as I took a random turn and then pulled over, waiting to see if someone might go past us.

"You caught that, did you? I told Chief Willson that I had to make a quick phone call and that my cellphone battery was dead. As soon as he was gone, I called time and temperature while I took a cursory look at the man's desk."

"Did you find anything?"

"Nothing," he admitted. "It was worth a try, though."

"No doubt." When no one passed after a reasonable amount of time, I turned the Jeep around as I asked, "Where should we go now? Should we head back to April Springs, since the police station was a dead end?"

"I still want to talk to Officer Durant," Jake said, "but he's not getting off duty for another two hours. I'm pretty sure that the chief wouldn't approve of me speaking directly to him, but that's not really a concern of mine after the way he just tried to snow me. Do you two mind hanging around town until then?"

"It's fine by me. How about you, Grace?"

"My calendar is wide open for the rest of the day. What should we do while we're waiting, though?"

"I thought we might all have another run at the suspects you spoke with yesterday," Jake admitted. "Would you two mind if I tagged along?"

"No, that's okay with us, right, Grace?"

"At this point I don't see what it could hurt," she admitted.

"Then let's go have a chat with your suspects. Who should we tackle first: Shannon Wright, Maisie Fleming, or Deke Marsh?" I asked so I'd know where to drive.

"Don't ask me. I'm just along for the ride," Jake said from the back. "You two decide."

"Let's tackle Deke first," Grace suggested. "He wasn't very forthcoming with us when we talked to him before, but maybe he will be now that we have Jake with us. Is that okay with you, Suzanne?"

"Deke it is. Do you think there's the slightest chance that he's back at that bar where we found him last time?" I asked.

"It's as good a place as any," Grace said as I drove there. "Maybe he uses the place as his office."

Once we arrived in the parking lot and got out of the Jeep, I told Jake, "Deke got out of prison a month ago, and Maisie Fleming told us that he's been hanging around the apartment complex where Alex lived before he took the job in April Springs. He was supposed to be in jail for three years, but we never heard why. Evidently the judge overturned his sentence because of something the DA did during the trial. I wonder what he did."

"You won't have to wonder for long. I can find out in thirty seconds," he said as he reached for his phone. I looked at Grace, who just shrugged. We usually didn't have those kinds of resources available to us, so why not use them when we did? After a quick conversation, Jake hung up, frowning. "Grant told me that he was in for assault, but he would have gotten out sooner if he'd kept his nose clean. He has a bit of a temper, though, and he got in a few fights inside."

"What's wrong?" I asked him. "You don't look very happy."

"I understand that Simpson has been looking for me," Jake said.

"Does he know that you're here?" I asked him.

"No, and Grant's not going to volunteer the information.

We should be fine."

I wasn't quite so sure of that myself, but there wasn't anything I could do about it, so I decided to drop it for the moment. "There's one more thing you should know about him. He told us that Alex had reformed recently, or at least was trying to. That's why he arrested Deke. He was trying to turn over a new leaf."

Jake's expression clouded. "He was probably lying." I knew my husband hated when anyone impugned the reputation of a law enforcement officer, especially one who wasn't around to defend himself anymore.

"He could be, but don't forget what Officer Farley said. She told us that half the force hated Alex, and she implied that it was more than a personality conflict."

"I'm still not going to believe a bunch of hearsay until I have some cold, hard facts."

"Even if it's coming from another cop?" Grace asked softly. I tried to warn her off from that particular line of questioning, but evidently she had missed all of my signals.

"Even then. Let's go talk to this guy," Jake said as he strode off toward the bar's entrance.

"Grace, just drop it, okay?" I whispered as we followed him.

"Suzanne, he has to at least consider the possibility that some of the cops on the Granite Meadows force are doing things they shouldn't be doing."

"He'll consider it, but we don't need to swat him on the nose with it, okay?"

Grace looked at me for a moment before she spoke again. "You're awfully protective of him, aren't you?"

"Hey, that's not fair. I look out for you all of the time, too," I said.

"Like that?"

"Grace, I love you both," I said.

"Equally?" she asked me softly.

"Sorry, but no. Jake's first, and then there's Momma, but you're solidly in third, so at least that's something." I wasn't about to lie to her, not about something that important.

Grace let out a breath of air and smiled. "That sounds about right to me. It's natural for you to defend your husband, and I'd be a little bit worried about you if you didn't, but you've got to let me keep pushing him if I think it's important. If you can't do that, I might as well go back home and let you two work on this case together without me."

"Nobody wants you to do that," I said hastily.

"That's fine, then." We both looked up to see Jake hurry into the bar ahead of us. Where did he think he was going in such a rush? After all, we'd met Deke Marsh once. We already knew what he looked like.

I hurried up to go in after Jake so I could steer him to the man we wanted to speak with.

To my surprise, Jake was already approaching the convict's table. How could he have possibly known what Deke looked like?

Before too long, I was going to have to ask him just that.

"You're Deke Marsh, aren't you?" Jake asked him as he loomed over the crook's table.

Deke wasn't all that pleased to see him, or us either, for that matter. Without answering Jake's question, Deke looked directly at us when he spoke. "I talked to you both before, so this is what I get in return? You go out and find a cop to come here and try to intimidate me?"

"I never identified myself as a police officer," Jake said.

"You didn't have to. I see you didn't have any problem finding me when you walked in, either, did you?"

Jake just shrugged. "Tell me about Alex Tyler."

"He was a heck of a fine fellow," Deke said, his voice heavy with sarcasm.

"This will go a lot smoother if you keep your lip to yourself," Jake answered. His voice had gotten softer, but somehow it was more intimidating as well. How did he do that? And more importantly, could he teach me? I sort of doubted it.

That attitude coming from a cop and from a donutmaker was clearly two different things.

Deke just shrugged. "Tyler arrested me, I got three long, my lawyer got me out on a technicality because of something the DA did, and now I'm out, just another law-abiding citizen."

"I wonder if that's true," Jake said evenly. "You've got to be supporting yourself somehow, and I don't see you as the type to have a regular job. How long will it take me to uncover your real source of income if I start digging?"

Deke thought about that for a moment before he spoke again. When he did, there was a certain air of resignation in his voice. "What do you want to know?"

"Who would want to kill Alex Tyler?" Jake asked.

It was one heck of a lead question.

"Take your pick. I've got a few friends he put away, but you need to look on both sides of the law, if you know what I mean."

"Are you talking about another cop?" Jake asked. It was clear in his voice that he wasn't going to stand for any nonsense. I had a hunch that the next thing Deke Marsh told us would probably be true.

But what he said next nearly floored me.

Chapter 16

"It goes higher than that. Try the police chief himself," Deke said.

Jake shook his head. "Come on, get real. Are you honestly trying to tell me that Chief Willson was in on Alex Tyler's murder?"

"Hey, don't take my word for it. The man had his hand out to look the other way when he was the deputy chief, and he hasn't pulled it back in empty-handed since he took over."

"I'm still waiting for proof," Jake said.

"If you can crack Craig Durant, he'll tell you that I'm not lying."

"Alex's ex-partner?" I asked.

"One and the same. Durant didn't take too well to Alex trying to reform, either. I heard him threaten the man once myself."

"I can't imagine any cop being stupid or careless enough to say or do anything incriminating in front of you," Jake said.

"They didn't know that I was standing nearby," Deke said with a shrug. "That's not all, though. I heard Durant tell Alex that if he tried to do anything about stopping what had been going on, he'd pay for it. Then Durant said that the chief would put him on a solo patrol shift at midnight in the worst part of town, and nobody would answer if he called in for backup. That shook Alex up pretty good from what I could see."

"What did he say in response?" Grace asked, caught up in this new revelation as well.

Deke shrugged again. "Beats me. I didn't hang around to find out. I knew if they found out I'd been listening to their little conversation, it was not going to end well for me, so I took off."

"When did all of this supposedly happen?" Jake asked.

"Three days before Tyler took the job in April Springs," the criminal said. "That's it. I'm tapped. I don't have anything else for you."

Jake stared hard at him before he answered. "I'm not ready to concede that just yet. We'll see you around, Deke."

"I'm not going anywhere," the crook said as Jake, Grace, and I walked out into the late-afternoon light. The sky was gray, heavy with snow; at least that's how it looked to me. Maybe I was just a little paranoid about us getting enough accumulation to matter.

"Wow, that was quite a different conversation than the one we had with him," Grace said. Before I could ask my question, Grace asked it for me. "How did you even know that was Deke Marsh? We never pointed him out to you."

"Did you see the way he nursed that drink? He had his forearm around it, as though he were guarding it from being taken. That's a jailhouse move if ever there was one. I took a shot the second I saw that."

"Good to know," Grace said. "I'm sorry that it looks as though the police chief here might be involved."

"We don't know that!" Jake lashed out at her.

"Take it easy, big guy. We're on the same team, remember?" Grace asked softly.

After a few moments, Jake let a deep breath out. "Sorry. I shouldn't have overreacted. I've just seen too many cops accused of doing things they never would have dreamed of doing. It can ruin a career if it's not true."

"And if it is?" I asked him as we approached my Jeep.

"Then they deserve whatever punishment they get, just like everybody else." Wow, some things really were just that black and white in my husband's mind.

"How do we find out if Deke Marsh was telling us the truth, though?" Grace asked.

"I'll ask around—discreetly, of course—but I have a hunch that if that man's lips are moving, he's probably lying. Let's move on to your next suspect." Jake glanced at his watch, and then he added, "We've got another hour before Durant is due back at the station."

"Then let's go tackle the ice queen," I said. "Honestly, I

want to see what Shannon Wright makes of you."

Jake smiled a little, something I was glad to see that he was still capable of doing, even if he was in his full investigative mode. "I'll be nothing but charming; I promise."

"Oh, I don't doubt that for an instant," I said, doing my best not to grin.

Grace was not equally restrained. Her smile was broad as she said, "She's a real piece of work. I can't wait to see this, either."

"She can't be as bad as the two of you are implying," Jake said.

"We'll see soon enough. We're here," I said as I parked the Jeep and we got out.

It was time for Round Two with the queen of mean.

"Hello, there," Shannon said when we knocked on her door. "My, aren't you a tall, handsome fellow." I could swear she was almost purring from the moment she saw Jake. I had to admit that I did not like the way she looked at him. While I'm not typically all that jealous, I was still a little uneasy about the way she focused so intently on my husband. It was as though Grace and I weren't even there. I'd wondered about the appeal she'd had for Alex Tyler, but that question had been answered now. When she turned her full attention on a man, it was almost radiant.

"Ms. Wright?" Jake asked.

"Please, call me Shannon," she said. "And you are?"

"This is my husband, Jake," I said, just to be sure that she knew I was standing there. From her lack of eye contact with Grace or me, I hadn't been quite sure.

Still ignoring me, she offered her hand to Jake. "It's a pleasure to meet you."

He shook it curtly, even though it was pretty clear that she'd been trying to hold onto it a little longer. "I'd invite you in, but the place is a mess."

I glanced behind her and saw that the apartment was immaculate, and I had a hunch that if Jake had been alone, the invitation would have been issued quickly enough.

"I'm sure that it's fine. We're here about your ex-husband," Jake said as he glanced at Grace and me.

"As I told your wife, I don't know anything about what happened to him," Shannon said. "I'm sorry you wasted a trip coming here."

"That's fine. We were already in town to coordinate with the Granite Meadows police department," Jake said, giving his voice that tone of authority he used so well. If I didn't know better, I would have believed him myself, but calling what we were doing with the local police cooperation was beyond any stretch of the imagination.

Hopefully Shannon wouldn't know that.

"It's all such a shock," Shannon said. "To think that someone would murder poor Alex."

"Where were *you* the day he was murdered? Is there any chance that you might have seen him?" Jake asked.

Shannon looked as though she'd been shocked by an exposed electrical wire when he'd asked her for an alibi. "Surely you don't think that I could have had anything to do with it."

"When a former spouse is murdered, we always look at the ex first," Jake explained calmly. "If you'll just tell us where you were, we can take your name off our list and be on our way."

"I was here all day, alone, I'm afraid," Shannon said after a momentary hesitation. Was she really a little hurt that Jake had asked her for her whereabouts, or was she just acting?

"Did you have any contact with anyone like a delivery man, a mailman, anyone?" I asked.

She glanced over at me for a split second and frowned, and I had to wonder if it was because I'd dared ask her a question myself or that I'd had the audacity to marry Jake.

"No one," she said, as if she were shooing away a pesky gnat. "I'm sorry I can't be of more help." Almost wistfully, she looked at Jake another full moment, and then she started to close her door.

"I have one more question," Grace asked, but it was too late. The door was already shutting.

"Sorry, but I really must go," Shannon answered as it shut completely, and we were faced with a closed door.

"Wow, I didn't think it was possible, but I like her even less than I did before," I said as we walked back to my Jeep.

"Why wouldn't you? She was looking at Jake like a starving man looks at a free meal."

"What are you two talking about?" Jake asked.

"Seriously? You didn't notice the way she was acting toward you?"

"Of course I did," Jake answered. "I'm not blind, but I don't think she was really all that interested in me."

"Were you looking at the same woman we were?" Grace asked him. "Because from where I was standing, she was practically drooling when she spoke to you."

"That's just because she thought she might be able to manipulate me," Jake answered. "This isn't the first time it's happened, and I'm pretty sure that it won't be the last."

"This conversation suddenly got more interesting," I said. "Care to share any other stories with us?"

Jake stopped and wrapped me up in his arms, and then my new husband kissed me soundly. "Suzanne, there's only one woman alive that I'm interested in, and I just kissed her."

"Okay. I've got it," I said with a grin.

"She was lying about something, though," Jake said after a moment.

"How do you know that?" I asked him.

"She hesitated in all of the wrong places," he replied.

"And that's it? That's all it took to know that she was lying?" I asked him.

"There were a few other signals, but that was the main one."

I touched his arm lightly. "Could it be possible that your former job made you more paranoid than the average man?"

"It's within the realm of reason," Jake said reluctantly, "but I still think she was trying to hide something from us."

"Then we'll keep digging into her alibi," I said, and then I kissed him again to show him that I had his back.

"If you two are finished acting like teenagers, we have a bit of a deadline now if we're going to speak with Maisie before we have to be back at the station to meet up with Officer Durant."

"Then let's go," I said, happy that Jake had taken a moment to reaffirm the way he felt about me. I wasn't generally that insecure, but Shannon's direct assault had shaken me a little, even though I knew better than to worry about my new husband's loyalties.

Hopefully Maisie wouldn't try anything so obvious.

But after meeting with her once and then hearing the stories about her, I wouldn't put it past her.

The only problem was that she wasn't there when we got to her apartment.

At least she wasn't answering the door.

"I don't think she's home," Jake said after Grace knocked loudly when the doorbell hadn't worked to bring her out.

"She could be in there hiding from us," Grace said. "It's not like she didn't try to do it before."

"Why would she do that?" Jake asked.

"She's an odd bird," Grace replied. "Wouldn't you agree, Suzanne?" she asked me.

"Let's just say that she's a unique individual and leave it at that. One thing is certain: we can't just camp here and wait for her to come out if we're going to catch Officer Durant."

"We can always come back later," Jake said, "but Durant is the real reason I came with you two this afternoon. Let's go back to the police station, just in case he comes back early."

"That sounds like a solid plan to me," I said as we made our way back to my Jeep. I glanced back before we left, but there wasn't the slightest flutter in Maisie's curtains.

Either she truly was gone, or she didn't want to take the chance of being seen peeking out her window.

"Should we go inside and wait for him?" I asked Jake as I drove into the police station's parking lot. The cars had thinned out some, but then again, it was getting to be later in the day. I was getting hungry, but we didn't exactly have much time to stop and get a bite.

"I think we should stay right where we are," Jake replied. "It would be better if we caught Durant out here instead of in the station. I'm not sure how the chief will react if he knows that we're not just going to take his word for things. Park over near those squad cars," he directed.

"We don't even know what he looks like," Grace said.

"There were some photos on the chief's wall of different groupings with captions, and I saw one man next to Alex in a couple of shots. Unless I miss my guess, it was Durant."

"My, that's some mighty fine police work there," I said with a smile.

"It's an old habit of mine to take in everything around me when I'm on a case. You never know where the next clue might come from."

"Good to know," I said.

Grace was about to say something when a patrol car pulled into the lot. "Is that him?" I asked before he even got out.

"Looks like it," Jake said as he sprang out of the Jeep.

Grace and I followed quickly, and I wondered what the police officer would think when he noticed the three of us hurrying toward him.

Apparently he lacked Jake's training, because he didn't notice us at all until Jake was practically right upon him. "You're Craig Durant, aren't you?" Jake asked as he extended his hand.

"That depends. Who wants to know?" Durant asked without taking it. He was a big man, dark and swarthy, and he looked as though he'd never backed down from a fight in his life.

"Jake Bishop," Jake said. "I'm investigating Alex Tyler's murder."

"Who are you with?" Officer Durant asked, clearly

warming up after hearing the new information.

"I was with the state police investigative unit until recently, but now I'm working with the April Springs PD."

Durant looked genuinely happy to hear the news. "That's great! I've been waiting for someone to start digging into my partner's murder. I begged to head up the investigation myself, but the chief wouldn't let me anywhere near it. He said that I was too close to everything, and if I got involved anyway, he'd suspend me, so what choice did I have? If there's anything I can do, all you have to do is ask."

I wanted to ask him for his alibi on the day of the murder, but I had a hunch that might be a question better saved for the end of the interview or coming from my husband instead of me.

Jake asked, "Did your former partner ever mention anyone with a grudge against him when you two were working together?"

Durant seemed to give that question some consideration before he answered. "That's all that I've been thinking about lately. I don't have to tell you that if you've been on the job very long, it happens. Unfortunately, Alex wasn't that different from anyone else. There were crooks with grudges and a bitter ex-wife. It just doesn't make any sense to me why anyone would want to kill him."

"Was there anybody in particular you have in mind?" Jake asked him. "Besides his ex-wife, I mean. I've already spoken with Shannon."

Durant nodded. "She's got her own set of secrets, but I don't think she's a murderer."

"What kind of secrets?" I asked him, forgetting for a second that Jake was handling all of the questioning at the moment.

Durant looked over at me, and then he glanced at Grace. "I'm sorry, but who exactly are the two of you?"

"I'm his wife, and she's our friend," I said.

Durant looked at Jake oddly. "Listen, I'm not trying to be a jerk or anything, but do you usually take your wife and her friend on investigations with you? Are you taking this seriously? Because Alex deserves to get justice."

"Their presence here doesn't imply *anything* about my investigation. I am one hundred percent committed to solving this case. Ask around. You'll find out that I don't rest until I find a resolution."

Durant shrugged. "I believe you, but that still doesn't explain why they're here."

"If you'd feel more comfortable speaking with Jake alone, Suzanne and I can go wait in the car if you'd like," Grace volunteered. It was really odd hearing that suggestion coming from her, but I knew that she realized just as much as I did that Durant might not talk at all if we were standing there.

"No, that's fine," Officer Durant said with a shrug. "I just wasn't expecting you, that's all."

"Can you give me any other names of folks I should be looking at?" Jake asked again, reminding the police officer that he was still waiting for an answer.

"Trust me, it's all that I've been thinking about since it happened. There's just one person that I can come up with that makes any sense at all," Durant said.

"Are you talking about Deke Marsh?" Jake offered.

That caught Durant by surprise. "Exactly! How did you know about him?"

"This isn't my first investigation," Jake said confidently. "He had a grudge against your former partner, didn't he?"

"We'd had a few run-ins with him before, but nothing major. Deke wasn't too pleased when Alex arrested him this last time, though. I was testifying in court about another case that day, so Alex was working alone when he collared him. The odd thing was that Deke acted outraged after it happened. It never made any sense to me, but Alex told me to just leave it alone, so I didn't dig any deeper, but if I were you, he's where I would start."

"Why do you think that he would feel that way?" I asked him.

"I have no idea," he replied.

Since he'd already said that he didn't mind we were there, I decided that it would be okay to press him a little myself. "We heard from a reliable source that you and Alex had a huge fight when he took the job in April Springs."

Officer Durant nodded. "I'll regret that as long as I live. Alex and I decided to celebrate his new job, so we bought some beer and started drinking back at his place just before he left town. I mentioned something about his ex-wife, nothing he hadn't said to me a thousand times himself, but this time he took offense. He told me that he would always love her and that she didn't deserve to have me bad-mouthing her. It was over as quickly as it started, but one of his nosy neighbors decided to call the police. Can you believe that? The chief came by, saw that we were fine, and he went on his way. Maisie told you about it, didn't she?"

"I'd rather not say," I answered.

Durant just chuckled a little softly. "You don't have to. That woman is a real piece of work. She was desperately in love with Alex, and he didn't have a clue. I think she might be a little off, if you know what I mean. As long as I knew Alex, he never gave her one reason to believe that she was anything special to him, but you would have thought they were in love to hear her tell it. Maybe you should look at her, too," he said as his gaze narrowed a little.

"Do you really think she might have poisoned him?" I asked him.

Officer Durant never got a chance to answer, though.

I saw movement back at the police station entrance, and when I looked to see what was going on, I saw Chief Willson striding toward us, and worse yet, he was accompanied by an officious looking man about Jake's age, clearly scowling. The stranger was a tall, willowy man, well over six feet, but if he weighed more than a hundred and fifty pounds, I'd eat a dozen donuts in one sitting.

"Let me guess. That's Manfred Simpson," I said softly to Jake.

My husband looked up, and I saw a grimace fleeing across his face. "None other."

It looked as though our investigation was about to take a turn for the worse.

Chapter 17

"Bishop, what are you doing here?" the state police investigator asked when he and the police chief got within ten feet of us.

"I'm just chatting with Officer Durant," Jake explained in his lightest manner.

"You were specifically told to limit your investigation to the city limits of April Springs," Manfred Simpson said officiously.

"I go where my leads take me," Jake said calmly. "You know that, Manfred."

"It's Inspector Simpson to you now that you've left the state police," the inspector said rigidly.

"Okay, I'll play it that way if that's what you want, *Inspector*," Jake answered sweetly. There was a hint of steel within his response, though. It was clear that Jake wasn't at all happy about his former associate's attitude, but he knew that if he reacted openly to it, somehow Simpson would get the advantage of him.

"Go back to April Springs," Inspector Simpson said. "If you don't do so immediately, there will be ramifications I guarantee that you are not going to like."

Without directly answering the order, Jake just saluted the man with two fingers, smiled, and then pivoted and started walking back to my Jeep.

"We're seriously not going to just give up, are we?" Grace asked gently as we moved away from the three law enforcement officers.

"Of course not," Jake replied. "There's no way that I'm going to let this go just because of Manfred, so I'm not about to stop now."

"How are you going to be able to come back here after what he just said?" I asked. "Can he really make things bad for you?"

"Let's let him think so for awhile, anyway," Jake said.

"I'm still going to pursue Officer Durant and Chief Willson until I know that I can eliminate them both as suspects or confirm their guilt, whether Manfred likes it or not."

"What about Shannon, Maisie, and Deke?" I asked him.

"Those three are all yours," Jake said. "Besides, I have two more suspects back in April Springs that I could use your help with."

"Are you ready to share those names with us yet?" I asked.

"Why not? Maybe you'll be able to add some insight to my investigation. Besides, you already know who one of them is."

"What are you two talking about?" Grace asked.

"That's right. I forgot to tell you what happened," I told Grace. "Apparently Alex arrested Brandon Morgan for speeding, and they got into a pretty ugly confrontation. Brandon popped in at the donut shop this morning to ask me about the state of the investigation, which was a pretty odd thing for him to do, given the fact that he was one of the protesters outside Donut Hearts when Lester Moorefield organized picketers to get me boycotted."

"Interesting. Who else is on your list, Jake?" Grace asked.

"Some man named Dallas Blake," Jake replied.

"Dallas? You're kidding. Dallas wouldn't hurt a fly," I said, surprised by his inclusion on Jake's list of suspects. "What possible motive could he have had to want to kill Alex?"

"I understand Tyler threatened to shut down his illegal gambling operation," Jake said. "I haven't had a chance to dig into it yet, but he's next on my list." Grace and I started laughing, something that Jake didn't find all that amusing. "Did I just say something that was funny?"

"It's not your fault. You haven't lived in April Springs very long. Dallas is a deacon at the church, and he sponsors a bingo game there once a month. The prizes are all donated from local businessfolk, and the proceeds go directly to care packages for soldiers. I give a dozen donuts every month myself. Did Alex really threaten to shut his bingo game down?"

"There was a report on Tyler's desk that says when he tried to issue a warning, Dallas tore it up and threw it back in his face," Jake said.

"I would have paid to see that," Grace said. "Dallas is ninety years old if he's a day, and the sweetest old man you've ever met. He's as unlikely a killer as you're going to find."

"I don't know about that. I still need to speak with him," Jake said.

"We can stop by his farm on the way back to town, if you'd like," I suggested.

"He's ninety years old and he still runs a farm?" Jake asked incredulously.

"Mostly he rents out his fields, but he's got a nice-sized garden he grows specifically to donate to the soup kitchen in Hickory. I heard him say once that he has family there, and he liked what they did."

"Is this guy really some kind of saint?" Jake asked.

"He's probably as close to one as you're going to get around here," I replied. "Dallas is a real character; there's no doubt about that."

"Still, I need to see him," Jake answered.

"Done and done," I said.

Thirty minutes later we were leaving the farm, shy one dozen donuts but heavy with potatoes and beets from Dallas's garden.

"So, what's your verdict now that you've met him?" I asked Jake.

"Until I get a new and pretty compelling reason to suspect him, he's going to the bottom of my list. That was a pretty sound alibi he had, wasn't it?"

"It's not every day that you get a priest *and* a pastor to both vouch for you," I said. "Should we call and confirm his alibi to see if they were really all together on the day of the murder?"

"I'll take care of it when we get back to town," Jake said. "In the meantime, I need to bring the mayor up to speed on what's been happening."

While he was talking to George on the phone, I said softly to Grace, "You know, I've been thinking about something. I really wish that we had some way to take pictures of our suspects without them knowing it. It would make things a lot easier, wouldn't it?" I glanced over at an unusually quiet Grace. "Grace? What's up?"

"To be honest with you, I've kind of been doing just that ever since I got my new company cellphone," she admitted.

"Why didn't you tell me?"

"I really wasn't sure that it would work," she said. "Would you like to see the shots I've taken so far?"

"Not while I'm driving. Show me when we get back into town."

"Does that mean that you don't mind if *he* knows what I've been doing?" Grace asked me in an even softer voice.

"No, we're laying all of our cards out on the table now, remember? That was good thinking on your part."

"Thanks. I normally have one good idea a day, so I was glad I didn't waste that one," she answered with a grin.

As Jake hung up his phone, he asked, "What were you two just talking about?"

"Grace was just telling me that she managed to get a few candid shots of some of our suspects while we were interviewing them earlier," I said.

"Not bad. Is there any chance that I could get copies of those pictures?"

"Sure thing," she told him. "I was afraid that you'd be upset."

"Not a chance. If there's something the two of you can do to make my life, and my investigation, any easier, I'm all for it."

"What did George have to say?" I asked.

"He understands that these things take time. Oh, and he confirmed Dallas's alibi while we were on the phone."

"How could he possibly do that?" I asked.

"When I called, he was in a meeting with Father Randy about feeding the hungry in the area, and the priest confirmed everything we were told."

"So Dallas is officially off our list of suspects," Grace said.

"It appears so. That just leaves Brandon Morgan in April Springs."

"But we have a bunch left in Granite Meadows," I said. "Between Deke, Maisie, Shannon, Officer Durant, and the police chief, we've got more than our share there. There's no way around you defying the inspector and leaving all of them alone, is there?"

"None that I can see," Jake agreed. "I'll try not to be so overt about it next time, though. There's no sense ruffling his feathers any more than I have to."

From beside me, Grace said, "It's really amazing how many enemies Alex Tyler made in his lifetime, isn't it?"

"I guess he just had that way about him," I said, feeling a little guilty that the two of us hadn't gotten along in the short time that we'd known each other. I wouldn't have minded nearly so much if he were still alive, but the fact that things would never be right between us bugged me on a level that I didn't completely understand myself.

"That means that we've sure got our work cut out for us finding the killer," Grace said.

"You realize that you can still back out of our investigation any time that you want to," I told her.

"Are you kidding? Why would I stop when things are just getting more interesting? You know me, Suzanne. I'm in it until the end."

"Thanks," I said. "What do we do in the meantime, though?"

"We keep heading back to April Springs," Jake said.

"Is anyone else hungry?" Grace asked.

"I could eat," I admitted, leaving out the fact that I'd been thinking about food for some time. "How about you, Jake?"

"I've been so focused on the investigation that I didn't even realize that I was getting hungry myself."

"Believe me, I'm *never* that focused," I said with a grin.

"Then let's get a bite to eat on the way back to town. Anyone have any suggestions?"

"I say we go to the Boxcar," Grace said. "The restaurants and cafes between here and April Springs are nothing to write home about, and we can always count on Trish Granger to serve up something good."

"Can you wait that long?" Jake asked me.

"I'll manage," I said. "Besides, if we can't hold out without a snack, don't forget that there are a few more donuts in back. We gave away two dozen, but there should be another dozen left."

"To be honest with you, I completely forgot about them, too," Jake said.

"If I had your focus, I'd weigh twenty pounds less; I'm sure of it," I said.

"Don't you lose an ounce," Jake said happily. "I love you just the way you are."

Chapter 18

"Hey, Trish," I said as the three of us walked into the Boxcar Grill. It was my favorite place in April Springs to eat and my second favorite in our part of North Carolina, the first being Napoli's in Union Square. As I looked into the crowded dining car, I asked, "Do you have room for us?"

"If a table's not free right now, I'll make sure that one opens up," she said with a grin.

Trish had thrown out patrons to make room for us to eat there in the past, but I didn't want her alienating any customers. "Don't evict anybody on our account. We can wait," I offered.

"Nonsense," the diner owner said as she started toward a table of older men who were notorious lingerers. Fortunately, they didn't need to be told that it was time to move on. The second they saw Trish heading their way—her blonde ponytail bobbing with every step—they threw their tips onto the table and met her halfway. Trish turned back to us and smiled. "Look at that. Can you imagine? A table just opened up. I'll get it cleared for you, and you'll be all set." Then she looked at the three gentlemen who'd so recently deserted their spot and added, "I'll be with you all in a second."

"Take your time."

"No hurry."

"We've got all evening," the third one said.

Trish laughed as she worked quickly to clear away the dishes and wipe the table down. In a few moments, it was ready for us, and we gladly took our seats.

After we ordered, I was surprised to see our interim police chief, not to mention Grace's boyfriend, Stephen Grant, hurry into the diner.

"Chief, we're over here," I said as I waved to him. "Join us."

"Thanks," he said as he approached and gave Grace a quick

and rather self-conscious peck on the cheek.

"Come on. You can do better than that," Grace said as she grabbed his ears and planted a solid kiss on his lips this time.

There were a few anonymous cheers coming from other diner patrons, and I noticed the chief's cheeks redden slightly as he pulled away. "Grace, what did we say about public displays of affection?"

"That the more, the better?" she asked, and then she grinned. "No, I know that's not it. Give me a second. I'll remember."

"You might as well give up, Chief," I said. "She's never going to change. Should we get Trish over here to take your order, too?"

"Actually, I came in here to speak with Jake when I saw your Jeep parked out front," Chief Grant said as he took the empty seat between Grace and Jake.

I looked at Grace. "Did that sound a little ominous to you, or was it just me?"

"No, something's definitely amiss."

"Let me guess," Jake said. "Inspector Simpson instructed you to give me a stern talking to. Is that it?"

Chief Grant smiled slightly. "Something to that effect, yes. I was told to be firm in telling you that you overstepped your bounds today, not to mention your jurisdiction, even if I had to clamp down hard on you to make it stick."

"Consider me properly chastised," Jake said with the hint of a smile himself. "We've actually made some progress. Do you want to hear about it?"

Chief Grant grinned at Grace and me. "Since when did you team up with these two? Is that what the mayor had in mind when he named you as his special investigator?"

"Seeing that George worked with them before he even became mayor, I was ordered to take their suggestions, and any help they cared to give me, willingly and enthusiastically," Jake replied.

"The mayor said that about us? Remind me to hug him later," I told Grace.

"We should make a George sandwich. He can be the stuffing, and we'll be the slices of bread," Grace replied.

"When you two are finished, we have some things to discuss," Jake said firmly.

I winked at Grace, and then I pretended to zip my mouth shut while she did the same.

"You were saying?" the interim chief asked.

"So far, we've eliminated one of our suspects in April Springs, and we've got five more in Granite Meadows," Jake reported.

"Five! How many people wanted him dead?"

"That's just how many we've found so far," Jake said. "If you want more than that, you're going to have to ask the two of them yourself, because they are the ones who uncovered the information."

Chief Grant looked at us both expectantly in turn, but neither one of us commented. "Well? Go on. I'm waiting."

I thought about giving him a hard time before I volunteered any information, but Grace took the decision out of my hands. "Shannon Wright is Alex Tyler's ex-wife, and a colder, more calculating woman I've never met. Deke Marsh is a crook Alex put away who just got out on a technicality, and Maisie Fleming is a woman who's been showing a little too much interest in the deceased for quite some time."

"Okay. I'm willing to admit that's quite a bit you've found out so quickly."

"There's more, but you aren't going to like hearing it," I said. "Jake, would you mind telling him yourself? It might be easier for him to take it if he hears it from you."

Jake shrugged, and then he spoke. "I'm reluctant to say this, but we've got reason to believe that his former patrol partner, Officer Craig Durant, or his chief, Robert Willson, may have been involved with his murder."

Grant studied Jake for several seconds before he spoke. "What reasons are those?" I had to give him credit. I knew that hadn't been easy to hear, even coming from Jake.

"From multiple sources, we've been told that Alex Tyler

took the chief's job in April Springs to turn over a new leaf and reform. That fact clearly upset some members of the force, apparently including the chief."

"So that's why you went with them today," Chief Grant said. "Because I'm willing to bet that no one would speak with them about the murder."

"No one on the police force, anyway."

"Did you have any luck yourself?" Grant asked him.

"Too little to amount to anything yet, but still too much to discount. I'm afraid that both of these men bear looking into, along with the rest of their list of suspects."

"You said that you've eliminated someone in April Springs. Is anyone here left on your list?" the chief asked him.

"Just one," Jake said. "A fellow by the name of Brandon Morgan. Tyler gave him a speeding ticket, and apparently it wasn't all that well received."

"That's hard to believe. I've written him up myself in the past for speeding, but he never came after me," Chief Grant said.

"I understand that, but I'm not willing to cross his name off yet without more of a reason."

Chief Grant nodded. "Nor would I expect you to. What's on tap for the rest of the day? Are you finished sleuthing, or do you have more folks to investigate?"

I glanced at my watch and realized that I didn't have that much time left before I needed to go to sleep for the night. "I think we're finished for today," I said.

Jake nodded. "No worries. We'll take it back up tomorrow."

"In Granite Meadows?" Chief Grant asked him solemnly.

"Like I told Inspector Simpson, I go where the leads take me."

The chief frowned for a moment, and then he said, "It's not going to make my life any easier, but I wouldn't expect anything less from you."

"Now I have a question for you," Jake asked him carefully.

"Do you honestly believe that your former boss could be involved in the murder?"

"No, of course not. Where did you get that idea?"

"From his wife," Jake said.

I nodded in confirmation.

Chief Grant shook his head. "I told him that folks were going to talk after the fight they had and that he should be ready for it. How did he take that as an accusation?"

"Does that mean that you don't suspect Emma or her mother, Sharon, either?" I asked him.

"Did someone say that I did? How do these things get started? I heard all about the rejection, but it never even crossed my mind that one of those ladies had anything to do with Alex Tyler's murder. Are you satisfied with that?"

"I am, but they may not be. I'll let them all know, though."

"You do that, why don't you," Chief Grant said. "I swear, being the police chief around here is not worth the pay raise." As he started to stand, Grace tugged at his sleeve. "Where do you think you are going?"

"Grace, I have a mound of paperwork on my desk. I might not be the permanent police chief, but until the mayor finds my replacement, I'll have to do."

"You still have to eat, though, don't you?"

The chief looked tempted, but I knew how duty bound the man was. He'd aged quite a bit over the last few months from the responsibilities of his new job, losing it, and then getting it right back, and I could tell that it weighed heavily upon him. I for one was glad that I didn't have that kind of responsibility. All I had to do was make sure that April Springs had their fill of donuts by the end of every day and then start the process all over the next morning while everyone else in their right minds was still sleeping.

"I don't know if I can spare the time," he said a little wistfully.

"Come on, stay," Jake said. "Trish will have you fixed up in a heartbeat."

"Let me ask you something. How many meals did you skip

while you were investigating a case?" he asked Jake sincerely.

"More than I can count, but then again, I never had the attention of not one but two lovely ladies, either."

"I should hope not," I said with a grin. "I thought all along that one was more than you could handle."

"And you'll never hear me say otherwise," he answered.

"I don't suppose twenty minutes will make a difference one way or the other," Chief Grant said.

A minute later, Trish showed up with four meals. "I figured you were staying when I didn't see you leave. Is this good enough for you?" she asked the chief as she offered him a plate.

"It's perfect. You're an angel, Trish."

"That's what I keep telling folks, but so far, nobody has believed me yet," she replied with a smile.

Between bites, Jake and I filled Grace and Chief Grant in on our honeymoon, sharing the funny stories and the romantic scenery we'd enjoyed in Paris. Grace interjected, showing off her euro coin, and Jake produced its twin and presented it to the interim chief.

"Smart," he said as he hefted the coin in his hand. "It makes for an easy gift, doesn't it?"

"And cheap, too," Jake replied with a grin.

I turned to Grace. "Men."

"Where is the romance in their souls?"

"That's okay. We've got plenty enough for both of them," I replied.

We talked of many other things during that meal, but none of them was murder.

All in all, it was the best time I'd had since Jake and I had come back from our honeymoon.

It was just too bad that I knew it couldn't last.

Chapter 19

"That was fun," I said as Jake and I headed back to the cottage alone. Even though we were all close enough to walk, Grace had insisted that the chief see her home, so the two of them had left together while Jake and I drove the short distance back to the cottage and settled in for the evening.

I was just getting comfortable when I realized that I couldn't remember if I'd turned the fryer off or not when I'd left that day. I'd only forgotten to turn it off twice since I'd owned Donut Hearts, but since then, I'd been in fear of burning the place to the ground with that hot oil boiling away all night long.

I kept trying to convince myself that I was just being paranoid when I finally asked, "Do you feel like taking a little stroll through the park?"

"I'd love to, but I'm still stuffed from dinner," Jake said. "How about a rain check?"

"That's fine. You stay right here," I said as I grabbed my coat. "I won't be long."

"Hang on. I'll go, too," Jake said as he stood and reached for his own jacket as well.

"I thought you wanted to stay here."

"I did, until I knew that you were going to go without me. Tell me something," he said as he zipped up his coat. "Are we just doing this for exercise, or is there a more practical reason behind it?"

"Can't I just want to walk around the park with my new husband and show him off to the world?"

Jake grinned as he answered, "You could if anyone else were out there, but we both know that the temperature's dropping fast, so the only people you'll be showing me off to are the squirrels."

"Okay, I give up. I confess. I can't remember if I turned the oil off when I left Donut Hearts today."

"Why didn't you say so? You know, we could always just

drive over. If you don't want to take the Jeep, we can go in my truck."

"Thanks for the kind offer, but I'm not sure that it will make it that far," I said with a smile.

"My truck will handle considerably more than a half-mile round trip," Jake said defensively.

"I'm sure that it would, but truthfully, I'd like the exercise. We walked *everywhere* in Paris together, and I kind of miss it."

"I do, too," he said, kissing me soundly before we went outside. As I locked the front door, Jake rubbed his hands together. "It feels like snow again, doesn't it?"

"This time of year, it always feels like that to me," I said with a grin. "I can't wait for you to see the park all draped in white. It's unbelievably beautiful."

"Especially when we're snuggling inside by the fire," he replied, though he still returned my smile.

"Walks in the park are magical, too. You'll see," I said as I took his hand in mine.

"I can't wait," Jake replied, and then we walked through the park, past the Boxcar, over the abandoned railroad tracks—which I happened to own due to a friend no longer with us—and to the front door of the donut shop. It was a microcosm of my life, that little walk, going from the house I'd been born in, walking through the park I'd played in as a girl to the shop I owned as an adult. It was amazing how much of my life experience had happened within a quarter of a mile, and if I added another mile to the radius, it would have taken up where I'd gone to high school and the apartment that I'd shared with my first husband, Max. Some folks felt restrained by living in a small town—at times my assistant, Emma, was one of them—but I found comfort in all of the old familiar places and things. I knew that I might leave April Springs someday if there was enough reason to, but it wouldn't be done without some very serious consideration. Too much of *who* I was was wrapped up in *where* I was, and at the moment, and for the foreseeable future, there was no place on earth that I'd rather be.

"This will just take a second," I told Jake as I unlocked the front door to the donut shop. "You can come in with me if you'd like, or you can wait out here."

"I'll come in where it's warmer," Jake said as he rubbed his hands together, and then I heard someone calling our names. It was the mayor. "On second thought, I'd like to chat with George for a few minutes. Do you mind if I do it without you?"

"Take your time," I said. "I've got some paperwork I need to go over in back. Just come in after you two are finished."

He kissed my cheek. "Thanks for understanding."

"You're most welcome," I said.

I was relieved to see that the fryer was off, and the oil was cold.

That didn't mean that our trip had been in vain, though.

I'd gotten a nice walk with my husband through the park in the deal, and that could never be considered time wasted.

I was still trying to figure out why I'd gotten two bills for one shipment of flour when Jake walked in smiling. "I take it your meeting went well."

"In ways you cannot begin to fathom," he said. "The mayor, without realizing it, just supplied me with an alibi for Brandon Morgan."

"How did he do that?" I asked, pushing my paperwork to one side.

"It seems that Brandon took up his speeding case with the mayor. He wouldn't stop arguing about it, so George thought he'd let the man talk himself out. It didn't work out that way, though. After Brandon finished complaining to the mayor, he started in on the town council, which happened to be meeting about loading zone variances. All in all, Brandon was in the mayor's presence the entire time in question. There's no way that he could have poisoned Alex's coffee and delivered it."

"How could anyone possibly know that?" I asked. "That

coffee could have been poisoned the day before the murder for all we know."

"The cup, you mean," Jake said. "It was coated with poison, remember?"

"Okay, the cup, and we both know that I'm not about to forget that. It's still true, though."

"The fact is that, based on the type of poison that was used, it would have become less and less effective pretty quickly if it were mixed in a coffee base. The lab said that Alex had to have been poisoned within an hour of its submersion in the coffee and that he hadn't been dead more than an hour after he was found. It gives us a pretty tight two-hour window of opportunity for the killer to strike."

"When were you going to tell me about that?" I asked, more than a little displeased with him for holding this particular bit of information back from me.

"Suzanne, I can't share everything I learn in the course of my investigations with you. You should realize that by now."

"I know, but I still don't have to like it," I said. "Why are you telling me now?"

"Because I just found out about it myself," Jake admitted with a grin. "George told me that the lab has been trying to get in touch with me all afternoon, but they didn't have my number."

"So you weren't withholding information from me after all."

"No," Jake said, "but just because I didn't this time doesn't mean that I might not have to do it in the future. My point is still valid."

"I understand that," I said. "You're in a real pinch now though, aren't you?"

"How's that?"

"Every last suspect we have left is from Granite Meadows," I answered, "and you're not allowed to go there."

"I am now," Jake said happily. "George worked something out with the mayor over there. Against Chief Willson's advice, I've been given permission to investigate there. There's a catch, though."

"Isn't there always? What is it? Do you have to work with Manfred Simpson?"

Jake scowled. "Not on your life. He can't touch me now that I have official permission to investigate there."

"Then what's the catch?"

"I have to keep Chief Willson informed of my activities and any results I may come up with during the course of my investigation."

"You actually have to keep one of your suspects apprised of your progress?" I asked. "That's insane."

"Even if it is, there's nothing that I can do about it. I gave my word."

"So, that means that you won't lie by omission, either, right? You're really going to tell him everything?"

"Yes, but there's a way around this," Jake said.

"I'm dying to hear what that might be."

"The truth of the matter is that I can't tell him anything that I don't know myself. If you and Grace uncover anything new that might be important, you're going to have to sit on the information until the very last second. That way I can honor my word and still track down Alex Tyler's killer."

"Let me get this straight," I said with a grin. "You're actually asking *me* to keep *you* in the dark?"

"On a limited basis, just this once, yes, that's exactly what I'm asking you to do," he acknowledged.

"I can handle that," I said, still smiling.

"Do me a favor. Just don't make a habit of it, okay?"

"I'll try not to," I replied as I turned back to my desk. "I don't know what's going on with my ordering system. I've got two bills for one delivery. I hate to think my supplier is trying to cheat me."

Jake glanced down at the two bills I'd been studying and flipped them over. After a moment, he said, "Here's your problem. This one isn't a bill."

"How can you tell?" I asked. I hadn't turned either one of

them over myself.

"It says right here, THIS IS NOT A BILL."

"Well, that's a pretty big clue, I'll grant you that," I said with a grin. "To be honest with you, that's a relief."

"Glad I could be of service," Jake replied. "Are you ready to go home now?"

"I am, and I've got to tell you, I really like the sound of that. Home has never sounded so good to me as it does right now."

"I know that I haven't lived there very long, but I'm pretty fond of it myself," he said.

After we locked up the donut shop, Jake and I walked back through the park to the cottage we now shared. It was definitely getting chillier, and I wondered if snow wasn't on its way after all. If it came, I'd do my best to be ready for it, but for now, it was time to settle in to what evening we had left before I had to go off to my early bedtime again.

It wasn't time just yet, though.

I planned to stoke the fire and snuggle with my husband a little first.

Chapter 20

When I woke up the next morning, I glanced out the window and saw that it was snowing again, but this time it was coming down more heavily than it had the night before. It was nothing that my Jeep couldn't handle, though. Still, if it kept up, we might be in for a bit of a winter wonderland, at least what passed for that in our part of the South. Jake's truck had four-wheel drive, so I knew it wouldn't be an issue for him getting around, either.

It was fun driving from the cottage to the donut shop, and instead of going straight in to work, I decided to tour April Springs a little in the darkness. The snowfall was reflected in the beams of my headlights as well as in the auras of the street lamps, giving the entire town a snow-globe feel to it as the barrage of flakes swirled ever downward. I drove around for about ten minutes instead of my normal forty-five–second commute, and then I decided to park closer to the entrance than I normally did. If the snow intensified, I didn't want to have to trudge through it to get to my Jeep.

Once I was safely inside Donut Hearts, the snowfall was lost on me as I started going about my day. Flipping switches as I made my way to the back door, I turned on the coffeepot, the lights in the kitchen, and then the fryer, in that order. It was already toasty inside the donut shop, and I was glad to swap my coat out for my apron. Emma had asked to come in a little late again, a request that I'd been happy to grant.

Before long, I had my hands in the batter of the coming day's cake donuts, wondering what I could do to be different and make my typical offerings stand out. Honestly, sometimes I felt as though I'd run out of ideas for making new donuts altogether. Over the years I'd made so many different varieties—and even more variations of old standbys—that it could be vexing trying to come up with something new enough to lure my customers for a sample.

Like anything else that required creativity, there were days when ideas flowed like water, but today, it was more like molasses. If I couldn't come up with anything new in flavoring, maybe I could decorate a plain cake donut a little differently.

Then it came to me. In honor of the snow falling outside, I'd make a snowflake donut. Drowning the first dozen plain cake donuts out of the fryer with glaze, I put an avalanche of shaved coconut on top. I'd never been a big fan of coconut myself, but it had its devotees, so I tried to keep something in the rotation for the folks who adored it. I had some glistening sprinkles that were new, clear sugar crystals that seemed to twinkle when they caught the light. Almost as an afterthought, I added a couple of shakes from the container to each top, and when I was finished, they were quite pretty, even if I wasn't about to taste one myself. It was a shame that I couldn't make them move, though, to take advantage of the special properties of my new topping. Truth be told, the sugar sprinkles were not nearly as attractive when they weren't moving. Then I remembered a revolving cake stand I'd gotten once on a whim. It would be perfect! I pulled the stand out of storage and plugged it in up front, right on top of the case near the cash register. Stacking the donuts on a clean white sheet of baking paper, I flipped the switch and watched the donuts dance.

I had just finished my homemade sign when I heard Emma at the front door, and I was curious to see what she thought.

"Snowflake donuts?" she asked in delight. "They're pretty, but why did you make them today?"

"Did it stop snowing already?" I asked as I looked outside. I'd been so preoccupied getting the display right that I hadn't noticed anything that had been going on outside.

"There's a dusting on the ground, but nothing new is coming down. It will probably all be gone again by the time we open."

"I don't care," I said with a grin. "I like the way they look, don't you?"

"They're actually quite lovely turning like that," Emma said as she took her coat off. "Who cares if we sell any?"

"Well, actually, I do," I admitted. "At least I know that I can count on selling at least two if Max comes in. That man loves shaved coconut. Maybe that's why I've never cared for it myself."

Emma laughed. "You could always call him and tell him we have them in stock today."

"No thank you. I haven't been in any hurry to see my ex-husband now that he's been completely replaced in my life."

"I'm sure that he'd be happy for you. I suspect that he and Emily will be following suit any day now."

"Why, has she said something to you?" I asked. While I was close with Emily Hargraves, my assistant was even closer.

"Not directly. It's just a feeling I get when I'm around them these days."

"Well, I wish them both the best if they ever do decide to tie the knot," I answered, and I was happy to say that I meant it. "I have another fifteen minutes to finish up the cake donuts, and then you can dive into the dishes."

"Sounds good," Emma said. "Thanks for letting me sleep in again."

"Hey, you can change your hours permanently if you'd like," I said.

"If I did that, I have a hunch that I'd have to take a pay cut as well," Emma said, her smile returning.

"Yes, there's always that. I'd pay you the same per hour, but there's no denying that you'd feel it in your check every two weeks."

"Then we'll keep things just the way they are now," she said. "Now get busy. I can't wait to get started on those pots and pans."

"I will, but in the meantime, you can get us ready out here," I said as I walked back into the kitchen to finish up the first part of my day.

Once I had all of our other, more standard cake varieties

finished, I came out and saw that Emma had embellished my sign with snowflakes and swirls of her own creation.

"Do you mind? I just felt as though it needed something," she said when she saw me noticing her work.

"I think it looks great," I said. "The dishes await you."

"Then I'll get right on them," she replied.

As Emma started washing, I began to work on the yeast donut dough. Soon enough it was ready for its first proof, Emma had done the first round of dishes, and we were ready for our normal break outside.

After we swapped out our aprons for jackets, we each got a cup of coffee and left the shop. I was a little disappointed to see that the snow had indeed stopped altogether.

"That's too bad," I said as I brushed the slight evidence of accumulation from one of the chairs we kept out front.

"You're not sad because we can't feature your new donuts, are you?" Emma asked me as we both sat on the cold chairs.

"It's not that," I said. "I was just hoping that it would at least cover the ground before it stopped."

"Suzanne, do you really love snow that much?"

"You know I do, but I had my own reasons this time. I wanted to take a walk with Jake through the park while it was snowing. It's the prettiest thing I've ever seen."

"Even prettier than Paris?" she asked, teasing me a little.

"Yes, even prettier, at least in my mind," I said. "Emma, have I been talking about my honeymoon too much?"

"Honestly, if you hadn't, I'd be worried about your new marriage," she answered. "It really does sound as though it was a lovely trip."

"I'm sure you'll get there someday yourself."

"Not if I have to wait first to find my own version of Jake," she said.

"What's going on with you? Are you in a dating slump, Emma?"

"Well, I hate to admit it, but it's been almost three weeks since someone new asked me out, so yes, I guess I am," she said solemnly.

"I'd feel sorry for you, I really would, but I had quite a few longer dry spells than that when I was single. You've got plenty of time to find someone."

"Oh, I'm honestly not in that big of a hurry. Hunting for a new beau is the fun part sometimes."

"Really? I always found it aggravating," I said.

"What can I say? I'm a gal that enjoys the chase." She jammed her hands deeper into her jacket and shivered a little.

"If you're cold, we can go back inside early," I offered.

"Not on your life. This is my favorite time of night, before anyone else is out besides us."

"I feel the exact same way," I said, echoing her sentiment. "That must mean that we're both in the right line of work."

"I hope so, because I'm not interested in a change at the moment," she said.

The timer I always carried out with me went off, and I stood. "Time to make the donuts."

"It never gets old," she said, and we went back inside.

"Thank goodness for that."

Soon enough, the outside chill was just a memory. I had my hands full of warm dough, and Emma had hers submerged in hot water.

For all either one of us could tell, it was summer outside.

But I knew better. I just hoped the snow came back to our little town, and soon.

It was a case of being careful what I wished for; I just didn't know it at the time.

Chapter 21

"What brings you to April Springs this early in the morning?" I asked the first customer to come through my door, a newly familiar face but a first-time customer, at least as far as I knew. "Were you in the mood for donuts all of a sudden?"

Deke Marsh scowled a little at my display cases. "Not particularly. What is that, coconut?" he asked as he pointed to my new snowflake donut special.

"As a matter of fact, it is," I said.

Deke looked at the one on top, shrugged, and then said, "Why not? I'll take one of those, and a cup of coffee, too."

Though he'd ordered something, the man was clearly there for more than my food. I just wasn't sure what that might be just yet. Still, a sale was a sale, so I rang him up, filled his order, and delivered it, along with his change. Deke took a bite of his donut, frowned a moment, and then he shrugged again. Was that the only way the man communicated?

"Well, what did you think?" I asked him curiously.

"Not too bad," he allowed. "They could use more coconut, though."

The only way I could have gotten more on top was by gluing it into place. "I'll remember that next time. So, if my donuts weren't what lured you here, what brings you by Donut Hearts this hour of the day?"

"Actually, it's late for me. The truth is, I haven't been to bed yet."

"Do I even want to know what you've been out doing?" I asked him.

"You might want to, but you're not going to find out, at least not from me. Listen, you need to pull your private pit bull off my case, okay?"

"Are you talking about Grace? I know she can be pushy at times, but she means well." I knew that he'd been talking about Jake, but there was no reason that I couldn't have a little fun with him, even if he was a crook as well as a murder suspect.

"We both know that I'm talking about your husband. I don't like him coming around asking me questions."

"Then answer them, and Jake will leave you alone."

"Let me ask you something? Does he really think I whacked Tyler?" Deke asked.

"You certainly had motive, just about anyone who didn't like him had the means, and the opportunity was there for the asking."

"Don't you sound like Nancy Drew?" he asked sarcastically.

It clearly hadn't been meant to be taken as a compliment, but that was how I was going to take it. "Thanks. She's wonderful, isn't she? Which book of hers is your favorite?"

"I've never read any of them," Deke said after snorting in disgust.

"You really should. They are excellent."

Deke shook his head as though this conversation was leaving him more and more puzzled. "What does he want from me? I've got the feeling that he won't believe me if I just tell him that I didn't do it."

"An alibi would probably help," I suggested.

"For when exactly, two or three days? Who has an alibi that will cover that kind of time frame?"

"Actually, they've narrowed it down quite a bit further than that." I wasn't at all certain that I was supposed to be sharing that information with one of our prime suspects, but how else could I get him to talk to me?

"I'm listening," Deke said.

I told him the time frame Jake had relayed to me, and to my surprise, he started laughing. "Did I just say something funny?"

"Hilarious," Deke said. "I couldn't have killed Alex Tyler, and even better, I can prove it."

"How can you manage to do that?"

"I was being hassled by his buddy during the entire time,"

Deke said. "If you don't believe me, just ask Craig Durant. He was busting my chops in Granite Meadows the entire time, so there's no way I could have poisoned Alex Tyler all the way over here. I gotta tell you, that's a real relief."

"Did Jake really bother you that much? How about Grace and me?"

"You two I could deal with," he explained. "It was your hubby I was worried about coming around and cramping my style. Let him know, would you?"

"You bet," I said. "He's going to want to confirm that, you know."

"Let him," Deke said. Then he wolfed down the rest of his donut, wiped his hands on his pants, and pointed back to my display. "I'll take three more of those for the road."

"Do you really like them that much?" I asked.

"What can I say? They taste better than they look."

If that were true, they must have been delicious.

I took Deke Marsh's money after I delivered his order, and the instant he was out the door, I grabbed my cellphone and called Jake.

After seven rings, I was about to hang up when he answered. "This is Bishop."

"I didn't wake you, did I?"

"No, I was in the shower. What's up?"

"I just got alibis for Deke Marsh and Craig Durant," I said.

I could hear the storm brewing in his voice as he spoke. "Suzanne, did you shut the donut shop down, leave April Springs, and track down two of our suspects without me? Please tell me that you at least took Grace with you."

"I didn't have to. Deke Marsh waltzed into the donut shop on his own. I guess I have you to thank for it, actually."

"How's that?"

"Well, it turns out that he didn't mind the questions Grace and I asked him, but when you got involved, he decided to end your interest in him quickly if he could manage it."

"What's that got to do with Durant?" Jake asked.

"It seems that the two of them were together in Granite

Meadows the entire time. Evidently Durant was hassling him about something," I said. In a gentler voice, I added, "I'm sorry, but I had to tell him the time frame of the murder. It was the only way that I could get confirmation from him that he was somewhere else at the time."

"That's fine," Jake said. "I knew that it would get out sooner or later, so at least this was for a good cause."

"What are you going to do now?" I asked him as I wiped the counter with a dishtowel I kept up front for just that purpose. Coconut flakes were everywhere, and I had a feeling that I was fighting a losing battle trying to contain them, especially since the coated donuts were making their rounds on the carousel display.

"I'm going to get confirmation that it's true, and then I'm going to strike two names off my list. Good work, Suzanne."

"Like I said, I didn't do anything. He walked into Donut Hearts of his own accord first thing this morning."

"Maybe so, but you saw an opportunity, analyzed the situation, and then you acted. That's pretty much all I've ever done in my entire career."

"Don't give me too much credit," I said.

"Isn't it okay for me to be proud of my wife?" he asked gently.

"It's more than okay, it's encouraged. Let me know if you find out that Deke was lying to me."

"I don't think he did. It would be too easy to prove, one way or the other. We're getting closer. I can feel it in my gut."

"Me, too. Are you still coming by after the shop closes this morning?"

"I'll be there. Is Grace free to go with you again?" he asked.

"She's making the time. So, we'll all meet up here a little after eleven and head off to Granite Meadows."

"In separate vehicles, though," Jake said. "I can't have you ferrying me around in your Jeep all the time, and the three of us can't ride all that comfortably in my truck."

"You could always upgrade to something nicer, you know," I said.

"Why would I want to do that when it's perfect for me now? I'll see you later."

"I'll be here selling donuts and solving crime, because hey, that's what I do," I said with a laugh.

"That's the woman I fell in love with," Jake replied before hanging up.

I wished that it really were that easy. I wasn't kidding myself. Deke had come forward because of the pressure that Jake's presence had put on him, not because of anything that Grace and I had done. There were some real advantages having a cop—one of any kind—on our side, and I wasn't silly enough to take the credit myself.

Still, we'd eliminated two suspects at once, and that was never a bad thing.

The only problem was that it still left us with three more: Maisie and Shannon for us and the Granite Meadows chief of police for Jake.

Frankly, at that point, I didn't have the foggiest notion which one the killer might be.

Chapter 22

"Suzanne, did you realize that you had a flat tire?" Grace asked me as she walked into the donut shop a few minutes before closing.

"What? No. When did that happen? It was fine when I drove over here this morning."

"Well, it's flat now," she said. "Do you need to call someone?"

"Call someone about what?" Jake asked as he walked in soon after Grace came in.

"I've got a flat tire," I said as I grabbed my cellphone.

"Who are you calling?" Jake asked me.

"Somebody to fix it. I can't drive around on a flat tire," I said.

"Hang up the phone. I'll take care of it myself."

"Jake, I'm sure you've got more important things to do with your time than change the tire on my Jeep."

"As a matter of fact, right now, that's my top priority."

I could tell instantly that I wasn't going to win this argument. For some reason, it appeared that this was a matter of pride for him. All and all, I was just as happy to let him do it. Honestly, it was nice having someone looking out for me. I threw him the keys and smiled. "The spare's mounted on back."

"I know where it is," Jake said. "I'll have it done in a jiff."

"As long as a jiff is less than twenty minutes, then we should be fine," I said with a laugh.

"Start the clock," he said as he left the building.

Grace started smiling the moment he was gone. "What's that smile for?" I asked her.

"I just enjoy having him around," she said.

"That makes two of us. So, did you manage to break free this afternoon, or do you have to go back to work?" Grace's job hours were flexible, but they weren't entirely fluid at times.

"I took the entire day off, so I'm all yours," she said.

"You didn't need to take the whole day," I protested.

"Are you kidding? I wanted to sleep in. The first half of the day was for me; the second half is for you and our investigation."

"Good. If everything goes as planned, then we should be able to get out of here as soon as Jake finishes changing my tire. Emma's already got most of the dishes, glasses, mugs, and trays cleaned and ready for the next day. I've got less than a dozen donuts left to deal with out here, a report to run, a deposit to make, and then we'll be ready to go."

"We don't have to sell all of the donuts first, do we?" she asked me.

"Of course not." I glanced at my watch and then added, "You know what? I think I'll go ahead and lock up. You can sit over there if you'd like. I won't be long."

"You know me; I don't mind sweeping," Grace said as she grabbed a broom.

It was different than when Jake had done it. For one thing, sweeping had been next on the list then, while I was nowhere near ready for it now. For another, Jake was methodical in everything he did, while Grace was more hit or miss, especially when it came to cleaning. I took the broom right back from her. "As much as I appreciate your offer, we have an order we do things in around here. The tables get cleaned first, the chairs get put up, and only then do we do the floor."

"Got it. Tables. Chairs. Floor. I think I can handle it."

She reached for the broom again, but I wouldn't let it go. Instead, I repeated, "Remember. It's tables, chairs, and then floors."

"I've got it," she said as she grabbed a dishrag and started wiping the tabletops down.

I was tired fighting her, so I flipped the sign to show we were closed and locked the front door. While I ran the day's reports, I looked in on Emma in back. "How's it going?"

"Almost got it knocked out. Is there anything else to do up front?"

"Just this," Grace said as she carried in the last tray that still held donuts.

"Hey," Emma said with a smile. "I didn't realize you were out there."

"I'm pitching in," she said proudly.

I managed to hide my smile from Grace, but not from Emma.

"Let me take that for you," Emma said as she reached for the tray. After depositing the last of the donuts into an empty box, my assistant slid the tray into the soapy water, cleaned it, rinsed it, and then put it in the rack along with the rest, where they'd be waiting for me in the morning. I used to put everything away at closing in the past, but Emma and Sharon had shown me that it made more sense just to leave things where they were more easily accessible the next morning.

"I'll be out front waiting and raring to go," Grace said.

After she was gone, Emma said softly and with a grin, "Funny, I didn't know that you were hiring extra help."

"Trust me, this is strictly on a voluntary basis." I looked around the kitchen and was happy to see that it was spotless. "You may have to do things over out front tomorrow morning."

"Got it," she said.

"Well, everything looks good back here. You can take off if you'd like."

"Thanks, Boss," she said, and then she traded her apron for her jacket and scooted out of the shop.

I grabbed the box of leftovers and headed out front to rejoin Grace.

"Everything okay out here?" I asked her.

"Right as rain," she said. "Your cash register stopped working, though. Is that a problem?"

"No, it just means that the report is finished," I said as I tore off the tape. After comparing it with the cash in the till, I was pleased to find that it balanced perfectly. "We're good to go as soon as we lock up."

"Then let's roll," Grace said proudly.

I could tell in an instant that things hadn't been done they way that I preferred, but all in all, it was good enough. Besides, making things right again would give Emma something to do in the morning while I was making the cake donuts.

"Okay by me," I said. "Thanks for pitching in."

"It was my pleasure."

Grace and I left the donut shop, and then I paused outside just after I'd locked the door. "Hang on one second. I'll be right back."

"Did I do something wrong?" she asked.

"Not at all," I said. "I just want to make sure that I turned the deep fryer off. Jake and I had to come back over here last night so that I could double-check it. I'm getting forgetful in my old age."

"The scary thing is that you're not that old," Grace said with a smile.

"I'll be right back." I went inside, did a quick double check of everything, and saw that I'd shut Donut Hearts down properly after all.

"So, what was the verdict?" Grace asked as I rejoined her out front.

"It turns out that I was worried over nothing," I admitted. After the door was locked, I glanced over at Jake, who was standing there frowning at my tire. Had he not even changed it yet? At least the spare was beside it.

As Grace and I approached him, I said, "Listen, I know this isn't your forte, so why don't I call someone to do it for me?"

"Why would you do that?" Jake asked. "I just changed it myself."

"Then why are you scowling at my new tire?" I asked him.

"Mostly because it's anything but new. Suzanne, your spare is hardly better than your flat tire."

"It will hold, though, won't it?" I asked him.

"For a day or two, but we need to get you a new one. There's a problem with this one, too," Jake said as he thumped the extra tire with his fist.

"I know. It's flat."

"It's more than that," Jake said as he pointed out a three-inch slash on the side of it. "You didn't get this by driving. Someone intentionally slashed your tire."

"Why would anyone do that?" I asked him as I studied the thin, straight line that had split the rubber. "It doesn't make any sense."

"You said that Deke Marsh came by here earlier, right?" Jake asked.

"What? When did that happen? What did he want?" Grace asked her questions in rapid-fire order. I wasn't at all sure how she expected me to answer them as quickly.

"I'll tell you on the way to Granite Meadows," I said, and then I turned back to Jake. "He was here, but he was also delivering up an alibi. It wouldn't make any sense for him to slash my tire. Besides, who cuts only one tire? Everybody I know carries a spare. If you're going to send someone a message, you have to at least cut two."

"Maybe someone stopped him before he could finish the job," Grace said.

"Maybe," I said uncertainly. "This isn't going to stop me. You two realize that, don't you?"

"I never dreamed that it would," Jake said. "You both need to be careful today, though."

"Aren't we always?" I asked him.

Jake frowned, and then he said, "Maybe we should stick together after all. We can take my truck, since Grace can't really use her company car for things like this anymore."

"Jake, we both know that we probably have a better chance of getting there on my bad tire than in your truck," I said. "Besides, we need to split up. The police chief isn't going to talk to you with us around—he's already proven that—and the women aren't nearly as likely to talk in front of you. We really don't have much choice."

"Everything you're saying makes perfect sense," Jake said, "but that doesn't mean that I have to like it."

"There's nothing to worry about. We'll all be within a stone's throw of each other if any of us needs help," I said as I kissed him quickly. "Do you want to follow us, or should we follow you?"

"I'll go ahead," Jake replied. "You still have to stop by the bank, don't you?"

"It will just take a second, but you go ahead. That way we can see you broken down at the side of the road easier so we can pick you up and give you a ride."

"My truck has more miles left in it than your Jeep does," Jake said proudly.

"Only time will tell if that's true or not, but I can't imagine it working out that way. See you soon. You be careful now, you hear?"

"I was just about to say the same thing to you," Jake replied.

"Yeah, yeah, yeah, we'll all be careful," Grace interjected, clearly impatient to get started. "Let's just go already."

"We're going," I said, and after waving good-bye to Jake ahead of us, Grace and I headed toward the bank and then on to Granite Meadows. We needed to make something happen, and soon.

We were down to our last three suspects, and only two of those belonged to Grace and me.

If you looked at it one way, the odds were with us.

We just had to find a way to crack one of our remaining suspects.

Chapter 23

"Who should we tackle first?" I asked Grace as we drove back to Granite Meadows again.

"That depends," she said. "Do you have a favorite?"

"Are you asking me which one of them I like the best? Between Maisie and Shannon, it's not exactly a race. Maisie might be a little obsessed with Alex, but Shannon seems downright icy."

"I wasn't asking you which one you wanted to have over for a slumber party," Grace answered. "I mean which one of them do you think might have done it?"

"At the moment I'm leaning toward Shannon, but Maisie clearly has a touch of crazy in her. We can't forget the police chief, either. He could have done it himself to hide something he didn't want the world to discover."

"Maybe so, but as far as I'm concerned, he's Jake's problem now."

"You know, there's a real possibility that all three of us might be wrong," I said. "Someone else could have poisoned Alex."

"I refuse to consider the possibility," Grace said firmly.

"Why is that?"

"Suzanne, what good would it do us if that were true? Let's focus on the two suspects we have left on our list, let Jake handle the chief, and then we'll deal with more options later if they all turn out to be busts."

"Okay. I vote we talk to Maisie first," I said.

Grace looked at me, clearly startled. "Seriously? Do you really think the crazy lady killed him?"

"I'm not sure, but poison doesn't seem like something Shannon would use. If Alex had been run over by an SUV, then *she'd* be my likeliest candidate. If she were going to murder someone, she seems like the type of woman who would want it to be painful and messy."

"Wow, you have an even lower opinion of the woman than

I do," Grace said with a laugh. "Okay, let's go see Maisie. Do you think she'll actually come out of her apartment this time? She wouldn't do it when Jake was with us."

"Who knows? At least she answered the door for us before. I'm hoping when she sees that it's just us girls, she'll be more willing to talk."

"So, how should we approach her? Could we play good cop/bad cop?" Grace asked eagerly. "I love it when we do that."

"That's because you always get to play the bad cop," I answered with a smile.

"Why shouldn't I? I'm really good at it. Besides, nobody's ever going to believe that you're the bad cop. You're just not mean enough."

"To be fair, neither are you."

"Maybe not, but I can sure play ornery," she said with a wicked grin.

"There's no denying that, but I was thinking this time maybe we should both be sympathetic to her," I said. "If even one of us is mean to her, I doubt she'll open up, but if we both try to relate to her, she might."

"It might be tough for me to do, since it's kind of hard relating to a stalker who might have killed her obsession," Grace said.

"Is it? If we can't be empathetic with the killer, chances are that we're not going to catch one. We have to put ourselves in their shoes, and that means imagining how the murderer's actions could seem perfectly sane and reasonable to us from their perspective."

"Is that why you're so good at this?" Grace asked.

"Think of it this way. Do you remember how you fantasized about being with Bobby Westlake some day?"

"Suzanne, I was in eighth grade," she protested.

"I remember. That's all you talked about for an entire summer. How many notebooks did you fill writing 'Mrs. Grace Westlake, Mrs. Robert Westlake III, Bobby and Grace Westlake'?"

"At least four or five," she admitted. "But I was just a kid."

"I'm not beating you up about it. Bobby was really cute. All I'm saying is that you should try to put those schoolgirl emotions into a grown woman's psyche."

"I never really thought of it that way before," Grace admitted, and then she looked at me a little skeptically. "It's a little disturbing that you understand the way she feels."

"It's all about empathy," I said.

"I certainly hope so. How do we empathize with Shannon?"

"It shouldn't be that hard. We've both had bad relationships in the past. Just magnify them by a thousand, and that should tell us all we need to know about Shannon."

"There's more to it than that, though," Grace said. "If we're really putting ourselves in her shoes, we have to imagine that we're the center of the universe, and all mankind was put there specifically to serve us. When one of them fails to do so in a manner that pleases us, they must pay the consequences."

"That might be going a little too far," I said with a chuckle.

"Trust me, I've known women like her all my life. I don't think I'm overstating it one bit."

That thought made me shudder a little. "If you say so. Tell you what. Let's wait to analyze Shannon until after we speak with Maisie."

"Deal," she said.

The drive went quicker than normal this time, and I had to wonder if it was because things were finally coming to a head. I had high hopes that one of our three remaining suspects was the killer and that we'd be able to prove it soon. Maybe then the cloud over Donut Hearts would dissipate and we could all get back to our lives. It would be wonderful having Emma, Sharon, and even Phillip Martin out from under clouds of suspicion again, but the only way we were going to do that was to solve Alex Tyler's murder.

"Maisie, can we talk?" I asked as I knocked on her door yet again. It appeared that I'd been wrong. She was going to ignore us and hope we went away, which was exactly the way she'd acted when Jake had been with us.

If she thought that was going to happen, though, she was dead wrong.

"We're not going anywhere, and we've got all afternoon. You need to talk to us. We're here to help." I'd added that last bit in desperation, hoping for something, any kind of reaction at all that got us some face time with her.

"Help her? How are we supposed to do that?" Grace asked me softly.

I just shrugged.

And then the door opened.

The chain was in place, though, so we weren't inside yet.

"Help me? What makes you think I need any help from the two of you?" Maisie asked us through the partially open door. I knew the chain wouldn't keep us out if we really wanted to get in, but this was a mission of nuance, not a show of blunt force.

"The police are worried that you had something to do with Alex's death," I said.

Maisie's expression froze. After a moment, she asked softly, "Is that the man who was with you before? Was he a police officer?"

"He's investigating the murder," I admitted, glad for the opportunity to explain Jake's presence with us earlier.

"If he was with the police, then why were you two with him?" Maisie asked me.

I just wished that I had an answer for her.

Grace came to the rescue, though. "We thought that if we went with him, we could help you explain that you didn't have anything to do with harming Alex."

It wasn't the most rational explanation that I'd ever heard in my life, but then I wasn't the one Grace was trying to convince.

After a moment, Maisie asked, "You honestly did that for me?"

"We just want to help," I said. "Can we come in?"

"I'm not sure. I'm late for an appointment," she said, clearly lying.

"We won't take three minutes of your time," Grace replied reassuringly. My friend didn't give herself enough credit; she was a pretty decent good cop, too.

"Fine, but just three minutes," Maisie said as she closed the door, slid the chain off, and then let us in. "I'm sorry, but I don't have any coffee or tea to offer you."

"We can't stay long, anyway," I said. "Should we all sit?"

"I suppose so," Maisie said, and we entered her winter display again. "How can you help me?"

"We've been able to find out exactly when Alex was poisoned," I said. "All you need to do is tell us where you were at the time, and we'll turn the information over to the police. If you do that, then all of your troubles will be over." That was about as wild an overstatement as I'd ever made, but we really needed to find out where she'd been.

"Do you mean like an alibi? I know all about them. I read murder mysteries all the time."

"So do I," I said sympathetically. "That's exactly what we need." I told her the time of death, as well as the two-hour window previous to it that the killer had needed to poison Alex Tyler's coffee. "Do you have anyone who can vouch for where you were then?"

"Is that when it happened?" Maisie asked, and it appeared as though the woman was about to burst out crying. Once we were gone, she could relive her period of mourning for as long as she wanted to, but in the meantime, we needed an answer.

"It is," I said, reaching out and stroking her hand gently. "If you could help us help you, the suspicion about you will all be over, and you can mourn properly. Can you keep it together long enough to tell us your whereabouts?"

"I was getting my hair done," she said. "The complete

works: shampoo, color, and cut. Call Hair Razors here in town. Ask for Cindi. I can't believe that I was pampering myself while my poor Alex was being murdered."

She was starting to cry in earnest now, and I felt a bit like a cad, but we needed to get out of there, and fast. Otherwise we'd be consoling her all afternoon, and our investigation time was severely limited. "Is there someone you can call to be with you?"

"I don't need to. I'm taking my neighbor to the doctor for her appointment. She's always had a kind ear for me when I needed to share my problems."

"Then you should go speak with her right now," Grace said firmly. "We'll walk you over there."

"Okay," Maisie said, suddenly very pliant. I felt bad about dumping her on her neighbor, but hey, the woman was paying for her ride by listening to Maisie's woes, so that was something, anyway. At least she wouldn't be alone. I wasn't sure if I could abandon her like that if she hadn't had someone to talk to.

It just couldn't be Grace and me.

"Well, we can mark her name off our list," Grace said as we left the hair salon ten minutes later. Cindi had been working, and she'd confirmed Maisie's alibi.

It appeared that, at least for our part of the investigation, it had to be Shannon, or we were completely out of leads.

As we headed over to her place, I had to turn my windshield wipers on.

It was starting to snow again.

Chapter 24

"Shannon, we need to talk," I said when she answered the door to our summons. For once, the woman looked a little disheveled, as though we'd roused her from a nap. Good. Maybe her guard would be down a little.

"What do you two want?" she asked us with a snap in her voice. "Is it that dreary business about Alex again?"

"If you call murder dreary business, then yes, it is," I said. My patience for this woman was nearly exhausted. After all, how bad could her ex-husband have really been? I'd caught mine cheating on me, and yet we'd still managed to work out something civil between us, an odd sort of friendship, even. What had Alex's great sin been that his murder was treated so severely?

"I don't have much time or patience left for you two," she said. I had to wonder about her change in attitude since the last time we'd spoken. Was it because Jake wasn't with us? Did she truly only respond well to men?

"This will just take a minute," I said. "All we need to know is where you were at the time of the murder, and you'll never have to see either one of us again."

"You actually have the nerve to come to my home and ask me for an alibi? Good-bye," she snapped, and then she slammed the door in our faces.

"Well, that was productive," I said with a frown.

"More than you might think. Did you see what I saw?"

"I must have missed whatever you're talking about," I admitted, "because I didn't see anything."

"That's fine. While you were busy distracting Shannon, I had a chance to peek through the door and look around her apartment."

"What did you see?"

"There was a man's coat draped over a chair in the living room."

"How can you be certain that it wasn't hers?" I asked.

"The cut of it was obviously from a man's suit, and the wingtip shoes beside it just confirmed it. It appears that our suspect has male company."

"Why am I not surprised? I'm just not sure what good that information does us at the moment," I said. "It's not as though she was cheating on Alex with another man. They'd been divorced for awhile, remember?"

"I know, but whoever is in there might just be able to provide her with the alibi that she doesn't want to supply herself."

"What are the odds of that happening?" I asked.

"Suzanne, it's not as crazy as you might think. Alex was poisoned around lunchtime on a weekday, isn't that right?"

"Right."

"Well, it's around lunchtime on a weekday right now. Maybe our mysterious stranger was with her on the day of the murder. If we hang around, we might get lucky and be able to get an alibi out of him. What do you think? Is it worth a shot?"

"I don't see why not," I said. "Even if it doesn't pan out, it's brilliant thinking on your part."

"Thank you, ma'am. After all, I've learned from the best."

"There's one other thing, though," I added after a moment's thought. "Maybe we should hold back before we interview him, just to see what we can find out about the man before we confront him."

"Sounds good to me, as long as we don't lose him."

"We won't," I reassured her. "Now all we have to do is hang around and see who pops out," I said just as Shannon's door began to open.

There was nowhere Grace and I could hide to keep from being spotted.

It appeared that we were going to be having this particular conversation sooner rather than later.

"Chief Willson?" I asked incredulously as the police chief for Granite Meadows slunk out of Shannon's apartment still adjusting his tie. "How long have you been dating the wife of one of your officers?" I asked.

The chief shook his head. "I can't believe you two are here. Shannon warned me that you might still be lurking around in the shadows."

"We're not the ones sneaking around," I said. "Seriously? How long have you been fooling around with Alex's wife?"

"She's his ex-wife," he corrected me, "and I don't have to explain anything to you. As a matter of fact, we just started seeing each other a month ago."

"Is it every lunchtime, or is this one special?" Grace asked with a sweet smile.

"It's the best time for both of us to get together, not that it's any business of yours. Listen, no one knows about this, so you both need to keep your yaps shut, do you understand?"

"Chief, were you here the day Alex Tyler was poisoned?" I asked him firmly, ignoring his request.

He stared hard at me for a full ten seconds before he spoke. "Are you asking me for my alibi or Shannon's?"

"At this point, does it matter?" I asked him.

With a prolonged sigh, he finally replied, "We were together."

"Can you prove it?" Grace asked.

"We get food delivered," he said sullenly. "Mandarin Palace can confirm that we were here. Now leave me alone."

"With pleasure," I said as I stepped aside to let him pass.

He got into an unmarked patrol car and sped off, his tires squealing as he left.

"Can you believe that?" Grace asked me.

"I'm not all that surprised, given what we know about Shannon. It appears that she has a taste for police officers; she just traded one in for another with a higher rank. I need to tell Jake about this."

"Have him meet us at the restaurant," Grace said.

"To confirm their alibi?" I asked as I pulled out my cellphone.

"That, and the fact that I'm hungry. Why don't we kill two

birds with one stone and eat while we're there?"

"We might as well," I said, the resignation heavy in my voice. "We just lost our last two suspects. I don't have a clue where we should go from here."

Chapter 25

"What looks good to you?" Jake asked as he studied the menu. "I don't know about the two of you, but I feel like chicken." The snow was intensifying. Outside, through the window near our table, we could see the world fast becoming coated in white. The flakes were fat and sticky, clinging to everything they touched, and I was glad that we were in vehicles that could handle it.

"How can you think about food at a time like this? Aren't you the least bit upset that the delivery man just confirmed Shannon's and Chief Willson's alibis?" I asked him.

"Suzanne, if I let things like that interfere with my ability to eat, I'd weigh next to nothing, and to what avail? Starving myself doesn't help anyone."

"That's a man after my own heart," Grace said, and then she looked at her own menu. "I have an idea. Why don't we get three entrees and then split them?"

"Sounds good to me," Jake replied. "Suzanne?"

"Sure. Okay. Whatever you want to do."

"Wow, that wasn't very enthusiastic," Grace said. "Follow your husband's lead so we can all enjoy this meal."

"Well, if you two aren't worried about our prospects, then neither am I," I said. "Chicken sounds good to me. There are a dozen ways we can get it. How about you, Grace?"

"Chicken, in all of its glorious possibilities, sounds perfect."

Halfway through the meal, Jake said, "George isn't going to be too happy that we're back to square one. He was hoping that someone would have solved this case by now."

"There's always Manfred," I said with a smile.

"Don't even joke about that happening. If that half-wit ends up solving this case right out from under me, I don't know how I'm going to be able to look myself in the mirror."

"Would you have been that upset if we'd solved it

ourselves?" Grace asked him as she stabbed a piece of spicy chicken.

"No. If you two were to do it, I'd stand on the sidelines and applaud."

"What makes us different?" I asked him. "Is it because we're amateurs?"

"That's got nothing to do with it. It's because Manfred is an incredible idiot. You two are quite capable of investigating murder."

Grace looked at me and grinned. "My, those are heady words of praise, aren't they? I'm not at all sure that I've ever been called capable before."

"It makes your head swim a little, doesn't it?" I asked with a smile of my own.

"You two know what I mean," Jake said as he studied what we had left. "Should we get more rice?"

"No," Grace and I said in unison.

"Okay, I get it. Calm down, there's no need to shout," Jake answered. "Listen, I'm sorry we ran into a brick wall. Sometimes it happens, though. I'm not happy admitting it, but some cases never get a resolution."

"Don't say that," I said. "I can't stand the idea that someone is going to get away with murder."

"It happens more often than you might think," Jake said.

"Does it ever get any easier to swallow?" Grace asked him.

"I'll let you know if I ever manage to get past it," Jake replied as he pushed his plate away. "That was a good call on the rice. I'm stuffed."

"Me, too," I said as I pushed my plate away. "Grace?"

"I'm throwing in the towel," she said as her napkin landed on top of her plate. "Let me get this one, you two."

"We can pay our own way," Jake said as he reached for his wallet.

"Maybe so, but I'd like to treat my two dear friends to a meal out in celebration of their recent nuptials. You're not going to spoil it by getting all macho on me, are you?"

Jake took a deep breath and smiled, and then he put his

wallet away. "Thank you for a lovely meal."

Grace smiled broadly at him. "You know, you could teach Stephen a few lessons on graciously accepting the inevitable."

"He's still young. Give him time," Jake said, and then his cellphone rang. "Speak of the devil and he appears." As Jake answered his phone, he said, "We were just talking about you. Sure. Okay. Give me forty minutes. I'm in Granite Meadows. Thirty is the best I can do. See you there." After he put the phone away, he said, "I hate to eat and run, but the chief needs some advice on a case."

"What's going on?" Grace asked him.

Jake just shrugged.

"I know there's some kind of code you all follow, so I won't push too hard," Grace said. "All I want to know is if Stephen is all right."

"He's as good as gold," Jake said as he stood, and then he leaned over and kissed the top of my head. "See you tonight back at the ranch."

"It's a cottage, remember?" I asked him with a smile, and then I turned to Grace. "At his age, he gets forgetful sometimes."

"I'm not that much older than the two of you," he said, "so that's what you've got to look forward to in your near futures. Be careful going back. It's probably getting slick out there, and you're driving on one bad tire, remember?"

After he was gone and Grace settled up with the check, I said, "I can't believe we did all of that work for nothing."

"It wasn't nothing," she said as she pocketed her change after leaving a hefty tip. "We managed to figure out quite a few things about this case."

"Just not the identity of the killer," I said. "No big deal."

"Suzanne, even we can't win them all."

"Maybe not, but it's really frustrating, isn't it?"

"It can be. Now we need to get back to April Springs," Grace said.

"Why? Do you have a date or something?"

"I did, but evidently my boyfriend and your husband are going to be off somewhere together fighting crime, so my evening is suddenly free."

"You could always just hang out with me," I said.

"I must say, I've had more enthusiastic offers in my life," Grace remarked.

"I'm not going to beg. It's beneath me," I said with a soft smile.

"Since when?" she asked, grinning herself.

"You got me. I'd love to hang out with you, if you can make the time for me."

"For you? Always," she said.

We started to head back to April Springs, but long before we got there, something happened along the way that changed everything.

Evidently what we'd been doing hadn't gone unnoticed by everyone.

Chapter 26

I wasn't even out of the Granite Meadows city limits when I saw a flashing blue light behind me just as I heard the siren.

"What did I do?" I asked as I found a place to pull over. Jake had been right. It was getting slippery, and my bad tire wasn't helping matters any.

"Who knows? You surely weren't speeding; at least not in this mess."

Through the flakes, I saw the officer behind us get out and put on his hat. I knew immediately that it wasn't the police chief, since this policeman was in full uniform.

When I saw who it was, I almost wished that it was the ill-tempered police chief.

Instead, it was Officer Durant, one of my many former suspects.

"What's going on?" I asked him as he approached my Jeep. I'd had to unzip the window to do it, even though it was going to be a pain to zip up again. I'd been having trouble with it lately. To be fair, the whole Jeep had been giving me fits, and Jake had even had the nerve to keep suggesting that I replace it. It was rich coming from him, driving that beat-up old truck he owned.

"License and registration please," Officer Durant said solemnly.

As I dug into my wallet, Grace said, "You know full well who she is. This is harassment, plain and simple, and we're not going to stand for it."

Durant barely glanced at her as he took the offered documents and made his way back to his car.

Once he was out of earshot, Grace said, "He's just mad that we thought he was a cold-blooded killer."

"Imagine holding a grudge over something like that," I said to her.

"Do you honestly think that he's going to give you a ticket just out of spite?"

"I doubt that he'll go that far. I have a feeling this is just to tweak us both."

"Well then, he should consider it a success, because I'm fully tweaked now."

I put a hand on hers. "Grace, the worst thing we can do right now is to smart off to him. Let's just let him have his little victory, and then we'll get out of here once and for all, okay?"

"I'm not sure that I can promise you that," she said.

"But you'll try, won't you?"

"For you, I will," she said.

When Durant finally came back, I had to follow my own advice and not lose my temper with him. I was certain this was simply retaliation for us suspecting him of killing his partner, but I wasn't about to give him the satisfaction of seeing me lose my temper. "Is everything okay, Officer?"

"I'm sorry to say that tire doesn't pass inspection," he said as he pointed to my spare.

"I just had it put on this morning," I explained. "Someone slashed the original."

He shook his head without comment as he started to write something in his ticket book, and then, miraculously, he stopped. "Tell you what I'm going to do. I'll let you off with a warning this time, but get that thing fixed pronto."

"Yes, sir," I said, hoping against hope that Grace would remain quiet.

The cop made no move to leave, though, even though the snow was starting to come down quite hard. "I heard you had a run-in with my boss at Shannon Tyler's place this afternoon."

"Wow, word travels fast in a small town," I said as noncommittally as possible.

"You bet it does. You've got to be scraping the barrel looking for suspects if you went after the police chief."

"As a matter of fact, his new mistress was our main source of interest," I said. Where was this leading? I had no idea, but I was willing to play this game as long as he was.

I wasn't sure what to expect in the way of a reaction, but his smile still surprised me. "That's no great surprise. Everybody knows that the chief has been interested in Shannon for a long time."

"Even before Alex was murdered?" I asked.

"Long before that, if you ask me. Did you and your crack team happen to look at Tyler's crazy stalker, Maisie, like I suggested?"

"We spoke with her, but she had a solid alibi," I said.

To my surprise, the man actually looked impressed. "You two have really done your homework, haven't you?"

"We try," I said, "and once we get our teeth into a case, we never let go." It was false bravado on my part, but I wasn't about to admit that we'd hit a dead end.

"Do you have any other active suspects you're looking at?" he asked. "Maybe I can help. Or are you just giving up?"

"That's never going to happen," Grace said as she leaned over to stare at him, picking the absolute worst time to interject one of her comments. "As a matter of fact, we were just on our way to find Jake to share our latest bit of important information with him about the case. We expect to name the killer very soon."

Why was she lying to him? Was it a show of hubris, or did she just not like the way we were being toyed with? Either way, she needed to stop immediately.

"Listen, we don't have a lot of time. Are we finished here? We need to go," I said.

"What's your hurry? There's something you should both remember. No matter what else may have happened between us, Alex Tyler was my partner for six years," Officer Durant said. "That means something to me, whether you believe it or not."

"I have no trouble believing it," I said, doing my best to mollify him. "It was awfully convenient having an alibi, though, wasn't it?"

"I don't recall ever being asked for one," Durant said with a scowl. "What's going on?" He looked hard at each of us in turn, and then he asked, "Why did you need an alibi for me?"

"We weren't exactly looking for it. It just fell into our laps," I said, skirting the truth a little. "Deke Marsh told me that the two of you were together in Granite Meadows at the exact moment that Alex was being poisoned."

"He said that, did he? Well, it's true enough. I'm just sorry that I'm the one providing him with an alibi," Officer Durant said. "Otherwise, I wouldn't mind seeing him go away for it."

"Even if you know for a fact that he didn't kill your former partner?" Grace asked.

"Hey, he might not have done this particular crime, but I'm willing to bet that he's done a few things just as bad in his lifetime. After all, life's one big merry-go-round, and we all have to get off sooner or later." He tipped his hat to us, and then he said, "Be careful driving back to April Springs. We wouldn't want anything happening to you two on the way."

"Thanks. We will," I said.

I didn't even wait until he was back in his squad car to take off. I wanted nothing more at the moment than to put as much distance as possible between me and the townsfolk of Granite Meadows, including their law enforcement officers.

"Suzanne, what's going on?"

"He did it," I said as I sped away as fast as I could go. As I drove, I pulled out my cellphone.

"Who are you calling?" she asked.

"I have to tell Jake. You can listen to me when I tell him."

"We're in a dead zone, remember?" Grace reminded me.

"Maybe we'll get through anyway." I heard his phone ringing on the other end and prayed that he'd pick up.

Unfortunately, it went straight to voicemail.

"Jake, this is Suzanne. Grace and I are in trouble just beyond the Granite Meadows city limits sign on the way back to April Springs. Craig Durant did it. He killed Alex Tyler. If he gets us, too, you need to prove it. I love you."

"Suzanne, what are you talking about?" Grace asked as she

looked wildly backward.

"I may not be able to prove it, but I know it's true just the same. Craig Durant killed his former partner, probably to shut him up about his corruption."

"But he has an alibi," Grace countered.

"Sure, from a known felon who has a pretty big reason of his own to lie. That's what's been bothering me since I first heard it. We're taking a crook's word at face value that Durant wasn't in April Springs when Alex Tyler was murdered."

"And we don't have any proof that he was," she said.

"Not yet, but I'm willing to bet that we can turn something up now that we know where to look. Grace, how else could he have known about my bad tire?"

"He could have spotted it when he pulled up behind us."

"From that far away, with the snow coming down in thick sheets like it is? I don't think so. I've got a hunch that the only way he knew was because he's the one who slashed the first one, him or Deke Marsh doing it at his behest, anyway. That's not all, though."

"What else do you have?"

"Do you honestly think that the chief would go around bragging about his affair with a former officer's wife? He told us not to say a word about it, remember? I'm guessing Durant has been following us around Granite Meadows all day. He saw the chief leave Shannon's place, and then he saw us talking with Maisie. Why else would he follow us unless he wanted to see who else we suspected?"

"It's still not enough to convict him of killing his former partner."

"Did you take a picture of Durant with your cellphone?" I asked her as I struggled to keep the Jeep on the road.

"I got a few shots," I said.

"How much do you want to bet if we show it to Emma, she'll be able to identify him as a visitor to the donut shop that day?"

"She would have remembered someone in uniform, don't

you think? Hey, be careful!"

"I'm trying," I said. "What if he was in street clothes? I'm willing to wager that he bought that coffee for himself while staking Alex's new town out, and then he decided to poison his former partner."

"No offense, but it's all kind of based on some pretty sketchy reasoning."

"I'll grant you that, but we have some loose threads now, so if we start picking at them, something's going to unravel sooner or later. How long do you think his alibi is going to hold up if we start pressing Deke Marsh about it? How about if Jake does it?"

"If he's lying, couldn't Deke have committed the murder himself?" Grace asked as I continued to speed.

"He got out in a matter of days, remember? Deke might not have been happy about Alex arresting him, but it wasn't as though he paid much of a price for it. If Durant were on the take, though, the exposure would have ruined him, plain and simple."

Behind me, the patrol car was now following again, its lights and sirens going full blast.

"You're not going to pull over, are you?" Grace asked loudly as the Jeep's engine started to whine in protest from being pushed so hard.

"There is no way that's happening. I'll take my chances in court if I'm wrong, but I have a hunch that Officer Durant isn't trying to catch up with us to give me a speeding ticket."

"Suzanne, you'd better do something fast. He's gaining on us," Grace said as she looked back again. "We don't have a prayer in this Jeep."

"We just have to hang on long enough until we can attract someone else's attention," I said, doing my best to control my vehicle in the steadily worsening conditions. Where was everyone else? Most likely, they were safe at home riding out the storm.

I needed a witness, though, someone to keep Officer Durant from doing something to Grace and me.

If only one would appear.

It became a moot point a few seconds later. Going into a curve too fast for my Jeep's worn spare to hold, I felt myself losing control as I spun out and inadvertently headed into the woods. My vehicle had been built for off-road travel, but I was pretty sure this wasn't what they'd had in mind.

I had to do something, though, and it had to be fast.

If Grace and I were still sitting there like wounded ducks when Officer Durant arrived, neither one of us would make it out alive.

Chapter 27

"Suzanne, what are we going to do?" Grace asked, the fear thick in her voice. I'd never heard her as panicked as she was at that moment.

"We're going to be all right," I said as I tried to get the Jeep started again. The engine had died when we'd spun out, and I couldn't get it started again. "Grace, we need to go, and I mean right now."

"Start the Jeep and drive!" she shouted at me. "I'm not stopping you!"

"It won't start! Something's wrong with it!" I snapped back at her. "We need to go on foot."

"I can't! It won't open!" Grace started sobbing as she fought to open her door. I looked over and saw that I'd managed to wedge her side of the Jeep against a tall oak.

"Climb out my side!" I yelled. I threw my door open, but when I started to run, I quickly realized that Grace was still inside. On the road twenty feet away, I saw the patrol car skid to a stop. I was hoping at that moment against all hope that Durant would keep on sliding and wind up in a ditch himself, but his car was clearly better suited for the snow than mine had been. We didn't have much time to get away now.

"Grace," I hissed when I got back to the Jeep. "Let's go!"

"I can't," she said through her tears. "I'm stuck!"

I looked to see what was trapping her when I noticed that her seat belt was still buckled. Ordering her to free herself was clearly not going to work, so I leaned in and unsnapped it myself. Even once she was free, I still had to pull her out.

The siren suddenly died, and I turned back to see that the lights had been extinguished as well.

It became clear in an instant that he was coming after us, and he didn't want anyone else to follow him into the woods.

That could only mean bad things for us.

It looked as though my gut feeling was being confirmed by

Durant's actions.

The only problem—well, not the only one, but a big one nonetheless—was that Jake didn't have a prayer of getting to us in time, even if he had somehow managed to get my message immediately.

At least I'd been able to tell him that I loved him one last time, even if I hadn't been able to hear him say it back.

Chapter 28

"Come on! We need to go!" I told Grace as softly and as urgently as I could as I tugged on her arm. Once we were out of the Jeep, she just stood there as though she were in shock.

There was no response to my command other than gentle weeping.

I finally had no choice. I slapped her hard across the face, hoping that it would somehow snap her out of it.

It always seemed to work in the movies, but it didn't even make an impression on her.

Finally, I just grabbed her arm and pulled her along with me. At least she moved. The snow was coming down even harder now, and the temperature was dropping quickly. Could we use any of that to our advantage? I didn't see how as we plunged ahead together deeper into the woods. Grace was starting to respond now, and I had to pull less and less to keep her moving.

But where were we going?

I wasn't familiar with this area, and that might spell our doom. Was there a stream or something we could walk through so Durant couldn't follow our trail quite so easily? Even if there had been, wouldn't we be risking hypothermia wading in icy water? We weren't Marines, after all. I wasn't dressed for this kind of backwoods trek in the snow, but at least I had heavy denim blue jeans on, a thick sweater, and a decent coat on top of that. Grace was, per her norm, dressed more for style than for warmth.

I touched her hand again and could feel that she was freezing.

Without giving it a second thought, I pulled my jacket off and handed it to her. "Put this on, but keep moving as you do it," I said.

For the first time, I finally got through to her. "Suzanne, you'll freeze to death without your jacket."

"Are you kidding? I've got this toasty sweater on that

Momma gave me," I said. "You need it more than I do. Now stop arguing and put it on."

"Thanks," she said as her teeth chattered a little. As Grace slipped the jacket on, she looked wildly behind us. "Where is he?"

"I don't know, and that's what worries me," I said as we continued deeper and deeper into the thicket of trees. I looked back myself, but I couldn't see anything in the blinding snow. I'd read about people being lost a few feet from their doorsteps in blizzards, and I'd never understood how that could happen.

I was starting to get it now.

The snow was like a looming curtain of white, and it was everywhere, obscuring nearly everything within my vision. I could see the tree right in front of my face, but beyond that, we were just stumbling around without any real direction in mind other than trying to get away.

I was just starting to realize that I was missing my jacket more than I could have imagined, too. Its material had shed the snow as it had hit, but my sweater seemed to absorb it. I was quickly being weighed down from the heft of it, and things weren't going to get any better. This was going to have to be one of those times I suffered in silence, though. Grace had needed it more than I had, and that was the end of the discussion.

Had Durant given up on us? When I listened intently, I couldn't hear him anywhere in the woods around us, and with the snow coming down so heavily, I certainly couldn't see him.

Maybe we'd somehow managed to escape.

And that's when I heard his voice, much, much too close to us.

"Why are you running away from me, girls? I'm here to help you," he said. "What's gotten into you? You need to be reasonable, Suzanne."

I wanted to reply, to shout at him for doing this to us, but if

I did that, I'd be giving our position away, and it was the only thing we had working in our favor at the moment. I touched Grace's arm, got her attention, and then I held a lone finger to my lips.

She nodded that she understood, which was enough of a response for me.

"Do you think you know something that you don't? Is that why you're running? Why don't we go someplace warm and safe where we can talk about it? It's all just one big misunderstanding. We can clear it up in a second if you just give me a chance."

I kept Grace moving, but it was difficult not to make any noises in the underbrush. The trees were starting to get closer and closer together, too. Would this copse become so thick that our forward progress was stopped altogether? We couldn't go back now, and if we were forced to stop going forward as well, he'd have us. I couldn't think about that at the moment, though.

All Grace and I could do was keep moving forward, living one moment at a time, and hoping for the best.

"This is just aggravating me," he said, his voice closing nearer and nearer to us. "Trust me, you do not want to see me angry." After a moment, Durant spoke again, his temper clearly getting the best of him. "You were too smart for your own good. I knew you spoke with Maisie, Shannon, Deke Marsh, and even the chief. I didn't worry about any of them but Deke. He said something to you about me, didn't he? I knew I couldn't trust him. I'm going to have to take care of him after I deal with you two. Leaving him alive after he confirmed my alibi with you was a mistake; I can see that now. At least it's not too late to correct it."

Grace and I kept moving forward, but it was taking everything I had not to ask him the question that had been burning in my mind since I'd realized that he was the murderer.

Why had he killed his former partner?

Maybe if Grace and I could evade him long enough, he'd

supply the answer himself.

As we moved forward, I suddenly realized that it hadn't been my imagination.

The trees were definitely getting thicker now.

It wouldn't be long before Grace and I would be blocked as surely as if there were a solid wall of stone in front of us.

In an instant, I could see a bit of a break to the left of us. At least that's what I thought it looked like, but with the snow blinding me almost completely, it was hard to tell for sure.

Either way, we had nothing to lose by trying it.

I tapped Grace's arm and pointed in the direction where I'd thought I'd seen the opening. She nodded, and we moved to our left, hoping that there might be a break in the trees somewhere ahead.

Durant's voice returned, and it felt as though he was whispering in my ear he was so near. "I'm getting closer. I can feel it." He had to know that he wasn't going to get any responses from us, so why did he keep talking? Maybe he'd gone a little mad somewhere along the way. At least I hoped that he had. If he wasn't thinking clearly, then Grace and I still might have a chance of getting out of this alive.

"Might" was a pretty big word, but it was the only sliver of hope we had, and I planned on hanging onto it until it was gone.

"I probably should shut up," Durant said, "but what does it matter now? You're probably wondering why I killed Alex, aren't you? A part of me wants you to die not knowing, but who are you going to tell? After he busted Deke Marsh, he told me that his conscience was still bothering him. This from a man who had his hand out for bribes just as often as I did. What did he think he was going to accomplish wrecking both of our lives? I tried to talk sense into him, but he wouldn't listen. The fool gave me twenty-four hours to turn myself in, and then he said that he was going to do it for me if I lacked the conviction. I told him that he could go first, but he said that he had to make sure that I'd do what I said

I'd do before he told anyone about his own illegal actions. Our last conversation was the day that he died. I snuck away from work and drove to April Springs. I bet you didn't know that, did you? As soon as I left him in the park, I started wandering around town, wondering what I was going to do. That's when I stumbled across your little donut shop. I needed some coffee to help me think straight, but after one sip, I knew that it wasn't going to be enough to do the trick. I had to get rid of Alex, and I had to do it before he had a chance to rat me out. Why poison, you might ask? That one's easy. We took a refresher course on homicide techniques a few months back, and Alex had told me he'd rather be shot than poisoned. The idea of any kind of suffering freaked him out. Well, he didn't suffer long my way, but I knew that if I wasted a bullet on him, chances were good that someone might start digging into the time we worked together." After a moment's pause, he said, "Anyway, he took the poisoned coffee from me quickly enough, and that was that. I hit the inside rim with it to make it quick, but it was anything but clean." There was another moment of silence, and then he said in disgust, "This is getting old fast. If you both come out right now, I promise that I'll make it quick, but if you keep messing with me like this, I'm going to make you both feel some real pain yourselves before I end you." The threat was intensely real, and I knew that he meant every word of it.

And then things managed to get even worse.

The gaps ended completely, and Grace and I were solidly pinned against the trees. We could stand for a moment, but we couldn't go forward another inch.

It appeared that we'd just lost our last chance of getting out of this alive.

Chapter 29

"What do we do now?" Grace whispered. At least she was back with me, in full control of her senses. That was something, anyway. If we were about to go out, we were going to do it with our heads held high.

"Grace, there's nothing left for us to do. You don't have anything on you that we could use to defend ourselves, do you?" I asked her softly.

"There's some pepper spray in my purse, but that's back in the Jeep."

"That's where I keep my tire iron, too. Why didn't I dig that out before we took off?"

"You were too busy getting me out of there to worry about anything else. Suzanne, I'm so sorry that I lost it back there."

"Grace, listen to me. You have nothing to apologize for. You're the best friend I could have ever wanted. Thank you."

"Thank you, too," she said, the tears streaming silently down her cheeks again.

To my surprise, I touched my own face and felt tears there, as well.

"Let's at least get down on the ground and see if we can make it tougher for him to find us," I said quietly. There was a brush pile off to one side that might offer us some kind of refuge from the storm, if not from Durant. If we crouched down low enough behind it, he would have to be right up on us to see us. It wasn't ideal, but given the circumstances, it was the best we could do.

"I'm willing to try anything you suggest," she said as we lowered ourselves to the ground.

That's when I saw something that I'd missed standing up just a moment before.

There was indeed a slight break in the trees just behind the brush pile; I simply hadn't been able to see it before while I'd been standing up.

We wouldn't be able to walk out of the forest, but we might just be able to crawl out.

I pointed to the constricted opening. "Do you want to lead, or would you rather follow?"

"You go first. I'll be right behind you," she said.

I started crawling forward, hoping that this narrow little passage might lead us somewhere, but my doubts were beginning to come back as I realized that this tunnel might soon disappear.

If that's what happened, I decided that I could live with it. At least we'd both die trying to escape.

It might not be much, but it was all that we had.

Grace tapped my leg just as we came up against another dead end.

"Suzanne, could you use this?"

I looked back and saw that she had a broken tree limb in her hands about two inches thick and four feet long.

"How did you find this?" I asked as I took it from her.

"I accidently put my hand down on it in the snow," she said. "Will it help?"

"Like the man said, it couldn't hurt," I offered, and then I smiled at her.

"You can keep going now," Grace urged.

"That's the thing. I can't," I said. I had a sudden thought. Maybe I could distract Durant long enough to give us a chance to fight back after all.

I took off my sweater and instantly felt the chill of cold air and wet snow shoot through me. This was going to be pretty unbearable, but I really didn't have any choice. As I started to unravel the edges of my sweater, freeing the yarn into one loose strand, Grace asked me, "Suzanne, aren't you going to get cold?"

"If we don't do something soon, it's not going to matter much one way or the other. I just hope I can get enough yarn out of this sweater to make my plan work. If we can lure Durant deeper back in here and hide in that brush pile we passed, we might be able to fight back."

"At least take your jacket back," Grace said as she started to unzip it.

I wanted to refuse, but if I was frozen solid, I wouldn't be able to make this plan work. "How about this? We'll take turns," I said as I zipped it up, feeling the chill slowly start to dissipate.

I finally had all of the yarn that the sweater would yield in such a limited amount of time. I tied one end to a nearby tree branch shoulder-high, and then I carefully fed the material out as we started crawling backward out of the dead end.

It was our last hope, and it had to work, or Grace and I were dead.

"He's never going to see that," Grace said as she studied my rig.

"I know, but we can't put a jacket on it. The branch isn't strong enough, and in this snowfall, the movement is what we need more than the color."

"Why can't we have both?" she asked as she took her own thin coat off and tore at the lining. It was red with black swirls, something that should stand out in our current surroundings. "There, is that better?" Grace asked as she tied a piece of the sleeve's lining onto the branch where my yarn was attached.

"Much," I said. "That was a great idea, but we have to get out of here right now!" When she hesitated, I had to prod her a little. "Head back to the clearing, Grace."

"But won't we just be getting closer to him?" she asked me, the fear beginning to creep back into her voice.

I couldn't have that.

"Grace, this is our best and only chance of making it out of here alive. You want to at least go down swinging, don't you?"

"I'd rather not go down at all, but yeah, let's at least try to fight back."

We were finally back to the brush pile in the slight clearing, and I was relieved to see that I had just enough yarn left when I heard Durant again. The proximity of his voice made ice water run through my veins that had nothing to do with the cold that we were experiencing.

"Where did you two miserable witches go?" Durant shouted. I could swear that he was so close I could almost feel his breath on my neck.

It was time to pull the yarn and hope that it hadn't snagged somewhere between where I'd tied it and where I was now.

I saw the branch—and more significantly, the lining of Grace's jacket—move slightly with my tug, and then the yarn broke. Had Durant seen it, or had our ploy been in vain?

I could barely contain my glee when I heard him say, "Ah. There you are. Good-bye, ladies. I've got you now."

Then he fired three shots that appeared to hit where we'd just been.

If we'd still been standing there as Durant had hoped, he would have killed us on the spot, but as it was, he'd just managed to kill a tree branch that hadn't done anyone any harm.

I'd been right.

Durant had been closer than I'd realized.

Without hesitation, I swung the club out from my position as I crouched on my knees.

I'd hoped to break his leg with the attack, but the branch shattered as it made impact with his legs.

He fell to the ground, though, and his gun went flying in the process.

The odds still weren't in our favor, but at least we were in the fight for our lives now.

Chapter 30

I dove on top of him, and as I did, I felt some satisfaction that Grace was just a split second behind me. I used every dirty trick I'd ever thought about, clawing for his eyes, his throat, basically anything vulnerable that I could reach. I was proud that Grace fought equally hard.

Unfortunately, Durant was stronger than both of us combined.

The man threw us off as though we were rag dolls.

"You're both dead now," he snarled as he dove into the snow looking for his gun.

"Not if we find it first!" I shouted, and Grace and I scrambled for it as well.

Where had it gone? I was about to give up hope of ever finding it when my hand brushed against something, and I felt a moment of sheer joy.

It was quickly quashed when I realized that it was just another brittle, fallen limb.

When I looked up, I saw Officer Craig Durant standing over us, and worst of all, the gun was now back in his hand.

"I warned you. This is going to hurt," he said.

And then I heard the shot.

Only it hadn't been meant for me.

Or even for Grace.

As Officer Durant collapsed in the snow, a growing red stain spreading out from his chest, I heard Jake say, "Thank goodness we got to you in time."

As my husband was lifting me up in his arms, I saw Chief Grant doing the same thing with Grace, and I let the fear, the dread, and all of the anguish I'd been experiencing slip away.

Against the most imposing odds, we were safe.

Chapter 31

"I guess you got my message," I said as Jake took off his jacket and wrapped me up in it. We were all walking out of the woods together now that we had convinced the men that we were fine.

"We were actually on our way here to see Officer Durant when you called," Jake explained as he lent me his support. "It turns out that Alex didn't trust him to do the right thing, after all. He mailed a letter to his old boss explaining everything. There was enough in it to ruin him, and Durant, too. Apparently Alex knew his old partner better than anyone realized. I'm guessing that even his own murder wasn't entirely surprising to him."

"So then, does that mean that we just went through all of this for nothing?" I asked.

"Never believe that for an instant, Suzanne. After all, the two of you kept him occupied until we could get here," Jake said. "If you hadn't, there was a good chance that he would have been long gone. We found a bag of money in his personal car and two different passports, neither one with his name on them. My hunch is that he was getting ready to take off when you and Grace spooked him."

"Why didn't he just go, though? We wouldn't have been able to stop him."

Jake shrugged. "If I had a guess, I'd say that you managed to get under his skin. He wanted to settle one last score with you before he left. After all, in the end, you and Grace were the ones who uncovered the real clues."

"It still doesn't make sense to me, but the man was clearly nuts, so I'd probably go crazy myself trying to figure out his motivations."

"Trust me, his motive to get rid of his former partner was solid enough. I think he was on the edge before he killed Alex. After that, all bets were off. Durant saw an opportunity to go after you and Grace, and he took it."

"Is he dead?" I asked as I glanced back toward the body.

"He is. Don't worry about him now, though. We can talk about all of that later. Let's get you to a doctor first so they can check you out."

"I'm fine," I insisted for the hundredth time since they'd found us. "How's Grace holding up?"

"She seems to be okay. Why do you ask?"

"We had a rough time back there, rougher than I can ever remember," I said, shivering again.

"Well, it's all behind you now."

"Sure it is," I said. It turned out that we didn't have to walk that far before we came back to my Jeep. It had felt as though we'd trekked ten miles into the forest, but in reality, it had probably only been a twentieth of that.

"Is my Jeep totaled?" I asked him as I stared at it surrounded by the trees.

"Not even close. If you ask me, I think it will be easy to fix, if you still want to. You know, we can afford a new car for you."

"Thanks, but I like the one I've got," I said.

There was an ambulance parked beside Durant's squad car out on the road, along with Chief Grant's patrol car, too. A pair of EMTs rushed toward Grace and me the moment they saw us. "We're okay," I kept saying, but they continued to insist on fussing over us.

"Which one of you wants to ride in the ambulance, because you're both going to the hospital," one of them said.

"If we go, then we go together," Grace said, and I nodded in agreement.

"Fine, but we need to head out right now."

As we climbed in back, Jake said, "We'll be right behind you."

"See you soon," I said.

As we rode to the hospital, Grace squeezed my free hand that wasn't being monitored by the closest EMT. "That's it, Suzanne. I'm finished."

"Me, too," I agreed. "After we get back home, I'm taking a

long, hot bath, and then I'm going to sleep for a week."

"That's not what I meant," Grace insisted. "I can't go through that again. I'll always be your best friend, but I'm not going to investigate any more murders with you."

"We don't have to talk about that now," I said, doing my best to reassure her that we were going to be all right.

"Yes we do!" she said loudly, causing a look of concern to spread across the EMT's face as he monitored her vitals.

"You both need to take it easy," he said gently.

"Not until she agrees," Grace insisted.

"I do," I said. "Of course I agree. Grace, you've been wonderful. Thanks for everything that you've done. I get it. I really do. You're through."

"Are we still best friends?" she asked, the relief clear in her voice.

"The best," I said, and I meant every word of it.

We rode the rest of the way in silence, and I had time to mull over what Grace had just told me. Had she meant it, or would she change her mind in the light of a new day? I couldn't imagine investigating a murder without her, but then again, we'd just been through a pretty traumatic experience, and it had hit her much harder than it had me.

If she truly was done, then I was determined to accept her resignation gracefully, no pun intended.

I would always have her in my life.

Just not in my investigations.

Only time would tell, though.

In the meantime, I planned to celebrate every moment I had left as pure bonus time and to get every ounce of joy out of living that I could manage.

In the end, that was all that really mattered.

RECIPES
Oatmeal Donuts

These donuts might lack the flash and pizzazz of many of the rich and indulgent donut recipes in my repertoire, but there are occasions when what I want is comfort food, something warm and hearty without a lot of other ingredients. I save making these for those brisk, cloudy days when I have time to indulge in a recipe that doesn't have to be finished in mere seconds and there's no hungry crowd clamoring for instant gratification!

Ingredients
Wet
1 egg, lightly beaten
1/2 cup granulated white sugar
1/2 cup whole milk
2 tablespoons canola oil
1/2 teaspoon vanilla

Dry
1 cup all-purpose unbleached flour
1 teaspoon baking powder
1/2 teaspoon baking soda
1/2 teaspoon cinnamon
1/4 teaspoon salt

2 tablespoons oatmeal (old-fashioned, not quick)

Directions
Start by heating enough canola oil in a pot for frying to 360° while you work on the batter. While the oil is heating, in a medium-sized mixing bowl, beat the egg lightly, and then add the sugar slowly to the mix as you beat it with a fork. Next, add the milk, oil, and vanilla to the mix and stir. In a

separate bowl, sift the flour, baking powder, baking soda, cinnamon, and salt together—all the dry ingredients except the oatmeal. Add the dry ingredients to the wet, mixing lightly, and then fold in the oatmeal until the batter is smooth.

When the oil is at the right temperature, take teaspoons of batter and rake them into the oil with another spoon. If the dough doesn't rise soon, gently nudge it with a chopstick, being careful not to splatter oil. After two minutes, check the donuts for brownness, and then flip them one by one, frying for another minute on the other side until it is done as well. These times may vary given too many factors to count, so keep a close eye on the donuts.

Yield: Around a dozen small donuts.

Birthday Cake Donuts

There aren't a great many things I love about getting older, but having birthday cake on that special day is high on the list! I've tried on numerous occasions to top the standard white birthday cake in donut form, but I haven't been able to do it yet. I wouldn't say the icing is optional, not with my family, but the use of candles is strictly your choice. It's no one's birthday in your household, you say? Well, you know that it's got to be someone's birthday somewhere in the world, no matter what day you feel like making these, so choose to celebrate a perfect stranger's special day with your very own birthday cake donuts!

Easy Version
1 box birthday cake mix, your choice (we prefer Duncan Hines Classic White, but any boxed mix will do just fine)
1 cup water, lukewarm
1/4 cup canola oil
3 egg whites

1 container white icing (not optional, at least not for me!)

Follow the instructions for mixing on the back of the box, but to bake these, use your donut maker or a donut pan in your oven. The presentation is what makes these donuts instead of cupcakes, but hey, who are we kidding? They are delicious no matter what shape or form they may take.

Using a cookie scoop, drop walnut-sized portions of batter into small muffin tins or your donut maker, and bake at 365°F for 6 to 10 minutes, or until golden brown. Top with white icing while the donuts are hot.

Yield: 6–10 small donuts.

A Lovely Scented Donut

Suzanne may be a professional donutmaker in my novels, but I can assure you all that I am not. However, I do have the hearty enthusiasm that many other amateur bakers share, and I can't wait to experiment with new variations to my standard donut recipes. I stumbled upon this one on a rainy day with donuts on my mind, and after a few attempts, I found this combination perfectly delightful.

Ingredients
Wet
1 egg, lightly beaten
3/4 cup whole milk
1/2 cup white granulated sugar
1 tablespoon butter, melted

Dry
1 1/2 to 2 cups unbleached all-purpose flour, depending on desired consistency
2 teaspoons apple pie spice mix (cinnamon, allspice, nutmeg, and ginger)
1 teaspoon baking powder
A dash of salt

Directions
In a medium mixing bowl, beat the egg thoroughly, then add the other wet ingredients (whole milk, sugar, and melted butter), mixing until it is all incorporated. In a separate bowl, sift together the flour, apple pie spice mix, baking powder, and salt. Slowly add the dry ingredients to the wet, mixing well until you have a smooth, consistent batter.

Using two tablespoons, drop walnut-sized portions of batter onto a cookie sheet, donut mold, or in your donut maker, and bake at 350°F for 9 to 12 minutes, or until golden brown.

Yield: 8–10 small donuts.

If you enjoy Jessica Beck mysteries and you would like to be notified when the next book is being released, please send your email address to newreleases@jessicabeckmysteries.net. Your email address will not be shared, sold, bartered, traded, broadcast, or disclosed in any way. There will be no spam from us, just a friendly reminder when the latest book is being released.

Also, be sure to visit our website at jessicabeckmysteries.net for valuable information about Jessica's books.